"You seem awfully interested in what's going to happen with the sketch."

Ruth shrugged. "I just want Lily to find some closure."

Julian nodded. "I do, too. I'm hoping I can solve this once and for all. For her and for Jim."

"Thank you again," she said as they started walking down the street. The small parking lot of the restaurant had been full when they'd arrived, so Julian had been forced to park his truck on a small side street. Ruth hadn't thought twice about it at the time, but now that it was dark, she appreciated his presence. There weren't many working street lamps in this area, and the surroundings that had looked derelict in the light now appeared downright sinister.

"My pleasure," Julian said. "This has been really nice. Maybe we can do it again sometime?"

Ruth smiled and was about to reply when movement caught her eye. A shadow detached itself from a fence and began to approach.

Lara Lacombe earned a PhD in microbiology and immunology and worked in several labs across the country before moving into the classroom. Her day job as a college science professor gives her time to pursue her other love—writing fast-paced romantic suspense with smart, nerdy heroines and dangerously attractive heroes. She loves to hear from readers! Find her on the web or contact her at laralacombewriter@gmail.com.

Visit the Author Profile page at LoveInspired.com.

SILENT WITNESS

LARA LACOMBE

LOVE INSPIRED
INSPIRATIONAL ROMANCE

LOVE INSPIRED®
INSPIRATIONAL ROMANCE

Recycling programs
for this product may
not exist in your area.

ISBN-13: 978-1-335-63343-9

Silent Witness

For questions and comments about the quality of this book, please contact us
at CustomerService@Harlequin.com.

Love Inspired
22 Adelaide St. West, 41st Floor
Toronto, Ontario M5H 4E3, Canada
www.LoveInspired.com

Printed in U.S.A.

My heart is fixed, O God, my heart is fixed:
I will sing and give praise.
—*Psalm* 57:7

For my family,
with thanks for their enduring support.

Chapter One

"Miss Ruth? I don't think I can do this."

Ruth Becker stopped walking and turned to face the girl next to her. She knelt to the ground, ignoring the heat of the pavement against her knee, and looked up into the face of ten-year-old Lily Pushkin. The Arizona sun overhead was so bright it made her eyes water, but Lily deserved an immediate response. She'd been through too much already in her young life.

"Is everything okay?" Ruth asked quietly.

Lily darted a glance to her grandparents, who were standing a few feet away. George and Margaret Pushkin had raised Lily from the age of four, when her parents had been brutally killed during a home invasion. Lily had witnessed it all from her spot under the bed, and the trauma had rendered her mute. But thanks to the love and care of her grandparents, and a lot of therapy, Lily had started talking again. She was now a relatively well-adjusted kid, all things considered.

Until her nightmares had started nine months ago.

Ruth had begun seeing Lily at that point, using music

therapy as a way to help her work through the emotions of her nightmares. Ruth enjoyed spending time with all her patients, but her weekly sessions with Lily were special. There was just something about the girl that touched her heart, and Ruth always looked forward to their appointments. Lily was a sensitive, thoughtful child, qualities that Ruth found endearing. And her perseverance despite the losses she'd suffered in her young life was definitely something to admire.

Sensing Lily was worried about her grandparents overhearing their conversation, Ruth aimed a big smile in their direction. "Why don't you both go inside? It's hot out here, and Lily and I will be along shortly."

George and Margaret exchanged a worried look, but George nodded. Margaret looked like she wanted to protest, but she swallowed the words. "We'll see you inside, honey," she said as she and her husband walked past them, headed for the police station.

Ruth knew this situation had to be difficult for them. Lily's father had been their son, and they still grieved his death. Lily's presence was a blessing in their lives, but it didn't heal the pain of their only child's murder.

Ruth watched Lily's gaze track her grandparents. When her eyes flicked back, she knew they were inside.

"What's on your mind?"

Lily shifted on her feet, dragging the toe of one shoe across the sidewalk. "I'm just not sure I should do this. What if it doesn't help? It's been so long… I doubt the man is even still around."

Ruth nodded encouragingly. "That's possible. We've talked about this in our sessions. Do you remember what I told you?"

Lily sighed. "Any information is good." Her flat tone made it clear she was reciting Ruth's words from memory rather than genuine belief.

Ruth hid a smile at the girl's evident exasperation. "And what else did I tell you?"

Lily hesitated. "That I don't have to do this."

"That's still true." Her knee felt like it was on fire, so Ruth stood once more. "I know your nightmares have been bothering you. I don't know if talking to the police about your new memories of that night will make them stop. I don't think it will hurt to try." She reached out and brushed a strand of hair behind Lily's ear. "But I'm not going to make you do anything. You're in charge. If you want to talk to the detective, you can. If you don't, then we'll turn around and leave. It's totally up to you."

Lily looked down at her shoes. "It's not me I'm worried about," she said softly. She glanced up and looked past Ruth to the building beyond.

Realization hit, making Ruth's heart ache. "You're concerned about your grandparents?"

Lily nodded, her features scrunching with anxiety. "This has been really hard on them," she said, a hint of a quaver in her voice.

Ruth put her hand on Lily's shoulder. "And what about you, sweet girl? Hasn't this been hard on you, too?"

"Yeah, but…" Lily shrugged. "It's different for me."

Ruth tilted her head to the side, marveling at this display of courage. "What makes you say that?"

"I mean, it's awful. I hate the nightmares, and I wish I could erase my memories. But I'm learning to live with them, you know?"

Ruth nodded, and Lily continued.

"But my grandparents, they're old. And Grandpa George has a bad heart. They still cry about Dad, when they think I can't hear. They don't need to listen to me talk about that night." She shook her head and fiddled with the bracelets she wore on her right arm.

Ruth considered Lily's words. As a certified music therapist, Ruth was experienced in helping people deal with and process traumatic events. But she'd never had a patient quite like Lily.

The girl's concern for her grandparents' well-being was commendable and understandable. But Lily was her client, and Ruth felt obligated to do what she could to help her move through that and take care of herself. And right now, she thought the best course of action was for Lily to discuss her nightmares and the memories they'd dredged up with the detective assigned to her parents' murder case. Maybe Lily was right, and nothing would come of it. But Ruth figured that by talking to the police, Lily could better process her own emotions. The girl was putting on a brave face at the moment, but Ruth knew from their sessions that Lily was still hurting, too.

"It's very thoughtful of you to worry about your grandparents," Ruth said carefully. "But they want what's best for you. If you're concerned about how they might react to what you have to say, you can ask them to wait outside the room."

Lily jerked her head up. "I can do that?" She sounded uncertain, as though she didn't quite believe she was allowed to make that request.

Ruth nodded. "Yes. Like I told you, you're in charge.

If you want your grandparents to leave the room, that's fine. If you want me to leave the room, I will."

"No," Lily said immediately. "I want you to stay with me."

Warmth spread through Ruth's chest and she sent up a silent prayer of thanks. When Lily had first come to her, she'd been shy, timid and reluctant to communicate. She'd also been a little suspicious, thinking Ruth was going to be like her previous therapists. But over the last few months, Ruth and Lily had listened to music, played instruments together, and used movement and art projects to explore emotions. The unconventional approach had worked to draw the girl out of her shell and Ruth had earned her trust. It was a gift she treasured, one she was determined to protect.

Lily looked at the building again and sighed quietly. Then she glanced at Ruth and nodded once.

"Okay. Let's get this over with."

Together, they started walking toward the police station. The sandstone two-story building sat about fifty yards back on its corner lot, and the space between the building and the street was paved with bricks bearing the names of those who had donated to the police support fund. A forest of waist-high concrete posts dotted the area, making it difficult to walk in a straight line. Their presence made Ruth a little sad; Copper Cove wasn't exactly a hotbed of criminal activity, but nowadays nothing could be taken for granted.

Ruth held the door open for Lily, then stepped inside after the girl. A blast of cold air hit her, a welcome relief from the heat outside. Lily's grandparents approached, aiming worried smiles at their granddaughter.

"Are you all right, sweetie?" George asked.

Lily nodded. "I'm okay, Grandpa."

"You had us worried." Margaret's hand stroked down the side of Lily's arm. Her eyes were full of love, but Ruth saw the hint of tension on her face and knew the older woman was scared. And who could blame her? She thought she was going to have to listen to her granddaughter describe the murder of her son, an event that had forever changed their lives. She and George should be off enjoying retirement together, but instead, they were raising a child. Ruth had spoken with them both enough to know that they were grateful to have Lily, but she also realized this was an outcome no one had wanted.

"Sorry," Lily said softly.

"What do we do now?" George asked. He glanced around the lobby of the police station. At the far end of the open space there was a large desk; a doorway beyond led deeper into the building.

"The detective told me to let the desk sergeant know we're here." Ruth took a step forward, and Lily and her grandparents began to walk with her.

Just as they reached the desk, a tall man with dark brown hair and eyes walked through the doorway beyond. Ruth could tell he was a cop before she noticed the gun holstered on his hip and the badge clipped to his belt. There was something about his body language, the way he carried himself with a sense of readiness, as though prepared to respond to whatever he might encounter. His eyes scanned the room, assessing. When they landed on her, Ruth felt a tingle of awareness run down her spine.

Shaking off the reaction, she stepped forward, hand held out. "Detective Aguirre?"

He took her hand and nodded. "You must be Ruth Becker." His tone was no-nonsense, and a kernel of doubt formed in Ruth's stomach. Maybe this was a bad idea after all. Lily was still fragile, and if she had to tell her story to an unsympathetic listener, it could set her progress back weeks, if not months.

But the detective turned to Lily and smiled, and between one breath and the next, her worry faded. The expression transformed his face—he no longer looked unapproachable and hard, but friendly and even kind. Ruth breathed a small sigh of relief as she watched Lily smile shyly back.

"Hi, Lily," he said. Even his tone had changed, a note of gentleness entering his voice that hadn't been there seconds before. "My name is Julian."

He must have children, Ruth thought. There wasn't a ring on his left hand, but based on the way he introduced himself to Lily, Ruth thought he likely had a family of his own.

"Hello," Lily replied.

"Do you still want to talk to me today?" Julian asked. His body language was relaxed, his expression friendly and open. There was zero pressure for Lily to say yes— Ruth got the impression that if Lily changed her mind, Julian would accept her response with good grace and wave them off with no hard feelings.

She watched their interaction, her mind spinning slightly. When she'd spoken to Detective Aguirre over the phone, he'd sounded professional and flat. A hint of emotion had entered his voice when she'd told him about Lily's information, and he'd sounded eager to talk to the girl. But watching him here, she had to wonder if this was really the same man. Now that she was standing face-to-face with him, he seemed much more concerned with Lily's well-being than with the details she'd come to share.

Lily nodded. "Yeah, I do want to talk to you. But…" She trailed off and looked at her shoes.

Julian frowned slightly. After a second, he crouched down so that Lily was staring at him. He spoke softly to her, and Lily whispered her reply. Though Ruth couldn't hear what they were saying, she guessed Lily was telling him about her reluctance to let her grandparents hear her story. The fact that Lily was confiding in him like this, only minutes after meeting him for the first time, was a very good sign. Hopefully he would prove himself to be a man worthy of this child's trust.

Margaret sent Ruth a questioning glance. Ruth nodded and held up a hand, silently asking her to wait.

Julian stood again and stepped closer to the adults. "You're Lily's grandparents?" He introduced himself, shaking hands with George and Margaret.

"Is something wrong?" George asked. "Lily seems upset."

Julian shrugged one shoulder. "She doesn't want to talk in front of you. She's worried about how it will affect you both to hear what she has to say."

"That's ridiculous!" Margaret said. She glanced past Julian to her granddaughter, standing a few feet away. "We're not letting her go in there alone!"

"She doesn't want to be alone," Julian replied. He

indicated Ruth with a tilt of his head. "She wants Ms. Becker to stay with her."

Margaret's mouth dropped open, and she regarded Ruth with an incredulous expression. "But…" she sputtered.

Ruth's heart went out to the other woman. She cared so much about Lily, and she wanted to support her granddaughter, even though it was going to cause her pain. "Margaret," she began. "Lily is trying so hard not to hurt you."

"But I don't want her to worry about that!" Margaret interjected. "We're supposed to help her, to take care of her. Not the other way around!" Her voice trembled with emotion and Ruth stole a glance at Lily. Based on the girl's hunched shoulders, she'd heard every word.

"Maggie," George said softly. Margaret turned to look at her husband, her eyes brimming with tears. "We have to respect her wishes."

Margaret shook her head but didn't reply. She took a deep, shuddering breath, clearly struggling. Ruth sent up a silent prayer: *Please, help her. Let her find peace with Lily's request.*

Finally, after a long, tense moment, Margaret nodded. "All right," she said, her voice still wavering slightly. "I don't like it, but if that's what Lily needs right now, then that's what we'll do."

Thank You, God.

Margaret walked over to her granddaughter and wrapped her in a hug. She whispered something in Lily's ear, and the girl nodded. Then she released her and stepped back with a nod. "Grandpa George and I will be waiting right here for you."

Ruth glanced around the lobby, noting a lack of chairs or benches. As if reading her mind, Detective Aguirre spoke up.

"There's a coffee shop just across the street," he said, nodding toward the building entrance. "You might be more comfortable waiting there?"

George nodded and draped his arm around Margaret's shoulders. "That's fine. We'll see you soon, Lilybug."

Lily smiled at her grandparents. "Thank you."

As if by unspoken agreement, the three of them watched the Pushkins walk out of the police station. Once the doors had closed behind them, Detective Aguirre turned to glance at Lily and then Ruth. "Ladies, if you'll follow me?" He indicated the door beyond the reception desk with a sweep of his arm.

Lily reached up and took Ruth's hand. Ruth squeezed gently in a silent gesture of support.

"Okay," Lily said. "I'm ready."

Unbelievable.

Julian listened in awe as Lily described her memories in detail. He'd inherited this cold case after his partner, Jim Nelson, had died last year. The Pushkin murders had made the national news, and for the last six years, the identity of the killer, or killers, had remained a mystery, along with the true motive. A few things had been taken from the house, but not enough to suggest a robbery gone bad. Had someone been sent to assassinate them? Or had a threatening conversation escalated to the point of no return? Julian had still been in the police academy when the home invasion turned double homicide had occurred, and everyone had been buzzing with anticipation and a desire to bring the criminals to justice.

The story of Lily Pushkin, the four-year-old who had hidden under the bed that fateful night, had tugged on the nation's heartstrings. No one could be sure what Lily had seen, but one thing was certain—the trauma of the event had left the little girl mute for a couple of years. The fact that she was sitting across from him now, talking about what she'd witnessed and answering his questions, was nothing short of incredible.

She'd given investigators information before; Jim had briefly spoken to her a few years ago, but her grandparents had understandably been fiercely protective, so he hadn't been able to ask many questions. But now? Lily was providing the kinds of detailed descriptions that could make a huge difference in the case.

I wish Jim was here for this. Julian had worked hard to make detective after joining the Copper Cove police force, and he'd been partnered with Jim, a veteran detective who had helped Julian learn the finer points of his job. Julian had quickly understood that the Pushkin case was Jim's personal white whale, the case that had stuck with him and that he was determined to solve. Sadly, things hadn't worked out that way. One too many greasy burgers consumed on one too many stakeouts had been more than Jim's body could tolerate. He'd died of a heart attack last April, three years short of retirement.

Even though the Pushkin case had long gone cold, Julian had promised Jim that he wouldn't give up trying to solve the killings. In the two years they'd been partners, Jim had become a friend. He owed it to the man's memory, and the Pushkin family, to keep his word.

Still, he hadn't expected to speak to Lily Pushkin. He knew from the grapevine that the young girl was adjusting as well as could be expected to her new life. But Jim had always been very careful to respect the boundaries her family had set for her. His desire to solve the case was strong, but as a father, Jim hadn't wanted to risk retraumatizing her. His plan had always been to wait until Lily was older before asking her more difficult questions about what she'd seen that night, and Julian had been happy to follow his partner's lead. There was no statute of limitations on murder, and while the passage of time meant Lily's memories might fade, Julian felt it was more important that the girl find some peace.

So he'd been shocked to get that phone call from Ruth Becker. He still wasn't all that clear on what a music therapist did, but he could tell by the interactions between Lily and Ruth that this woman had helped Lily process her past. Lily clearly trusted her and saw her as a source of support. He'd been expecting to meet a fragile, small child, fearful and broken. Instead, Lily was tall, clear-eyed and brimming with courage. She carried herself with a degree of poise that some adults couldn't claim, and the longer he listened to her story, the more remarkable he realized she was.

He was glad Lily had asked her grandparents to wait outside. When he'd met them in the lobby of the building, he'd known by their expressions and body language they were barely holding it together. Hearing the details of the night their son and daughter-in-law had been killed would have been very difficult for them, and it would have made it harder for Lily to speak openly to him. As it was, she had struggled to share some of the things she remembered. But every time she'd had trouble, she'd looked to Ruth. With a gentle smile and a few soft words of encouragement, Ruth had helped her continue to speak.

Julian kept his attention on Lily, but in the back of his mind he wondered about Ruth. What was her story? How had she come to treat Lily? And what, exactly, did she do?

Even though they hadn't exchanged more than a few words, there was an air about this woman he found intriguing. She was pretty—there was no denying that. Her brown eyes shone with a combination of intelligence and empathy, and based on the faint lines at the corners of her eyes, she looked like someone who smiled often. She wasn't a thin woman—there was a softness to her body that was somehow comforting and appealing at the same time. For a brief second, Julian wished that he could hug her. It would be so nice to let go of all his stress and worry that way, if only for a moment.

Shaking himself free of the absurd thought, he concentrated on Lily's words. Nine months ago, the girl had started having nightmares. In these dreams, she saw the faces of the men who had broken into her house that night, and from what she was telling him, she'd witnessed her parents' murders.

"Can you describe them, Lily?" he asked.

She nodded and he took notes while she spoke. He was no artist, but she did a good job talking about the men, supplying details that her previous descriptions had lacked.

"I just have a few more questions for you," he said. Lily tensed, and he shot a quick look at Ruth. Ruth placed her hand on the girl's shoulder.

"Do you need a break?" she asked.

Lily shook her head. "No. Let's just finish this."

Ruth nodded at him, though her expression made it clear she didn't know how much longer Lily would be able to talk. Mindful of the girl's state of mind, Julian asked her questions about the actions of the men before they killed her parents—what they'd said, how they'd acted in the moments leading up to the murder.

Lily answered as best she could, filling in some of the details the original police reports had been missing. So far, she hadn't handed him a smoking gun in terms of clues, but he'd go over her responses more closely later. Hopefully, something she was telling him now would be the key to solving these murders.

There was just one more thing to ask before they wrapped up. "Lily, would you be willing to describe these men to a sketch artist?" If he had likenesses of the two suspects, it would make his job exponentially easier. Sometimes seeing a drawing of a face was all it took to jog someone's memory and help them come up with a name.

Lily hesitated and Julian held his breath. Was this it? The request that had gone too far? He knew it must have been incredibly difficult for Lily to talk to him today. Had he pushed her too much by asking her to come back again?

Lily looked at Ruth. "Do you think it will help?"

Julian bit his tongue, knowing the question wasn't for him. *Please say yes*, he pleaded silently. Lily would do whatever Ruth recommended. Surely Ruth realized how important this was?

"I don't think he would have asked you if it wasn't going to be useful," Ruth replied.

Julian relaxed slightly, but Lily still hadn't agreed. She frowned and looked down at the table, clearly torn.

He glanced at Ruth. She held up one finger, silently asking him to be patient.

After a long moment, Lily lifted her head. "All right," she said finally. "I can do that."

Julian nodded. "Thank you, Lily. I know this has been hard for you. I appreciate you talking to me today."

"When do you want me to meet with the sketch artist?" Lily asked. There was a note of anxiety in her voice, and he could tell she wasn't looking forward to the appointment.

"I'll have to look at their schedule," he replied. It was the truth, but it would also give the girl time to recover from their conversation today. He didn't know if it would be better for her to meet with the sketch artist right away, or if a longer break would be better for her. He watched Ruth as everyone stood and they headed for the door. She'd be able to answer that question, but it didn't seem like she wanted to stick around.

Julian led them back into the lobby, his thoughts buzzing. Lily's story had answered some of his questions about this case, but created many others. It was going to take time for him to parse through all this new information and figure out what was most useful. And he was very likely going to need to talk to her again.

He noticed the way Lily reached for Ruth's hand, seeking that connection. It was clear Ruth was an important figure in her life. Was she the key to understanding Lily? It certainly seemed likely. Which meant he was going to have a few questions for her, as well.

Lily's grandparents were already in the lobby, and they embraced the girl as she drew closer. Ruth hung back several feet, giving them space.

Julian walked over to her, watching the family reunion. "Thanks for your help today," he said quietly.

She jumped, and he realized she hadn't been aware of his presence. "Didn't mean to scare you," he said.

Ruth gave him a quick, embarrassed smile. "It's okay. I was just in my own head."

He nodded. "I do that, too." He turned to face her fully. "Listen, I'm going to have some questions for you. About Lily, and her treatment. Think you can talk to me about that?"

She slid a glance toward the Pushkins and bit her bottom lip. "That depends. I can answer any general questions you have, but I need permission from Lily and her grandparents before I'll give you any details about our sessions."

"I understand," he said. "Will you ask them?"

She held his gaze, a hint of reticence in her brown eyes. "Do you really need to know the details?"

Julian's respect for this woman rose a notch. She was clearly protective of Lily, and truth be told, he was glad of it. After everything she'd been through, the girl needed as many people in her corner as she could get.

"I'm afraid so," he replied.

"All right." Ruth nodded slightly. "I'll ask. But I'm

not going to push her to say yes. If she refuses, you have to respect that." There was a note of challenge in her voice, as though she was daring Julian to argue with her.

"Fair enough." He held his hands up, palms facing her. "I don't want to make this process any harder for Lily."

Ruth's body relaxed a bit at his assurance. "Very well, Detective. I'll be in touch."

With that, she turned and walked toward Lily and her grandparents. Julian hung back, watching her move. There was something about that woman that made him want to know more. Not just about the Pushkin case, but her as a person. He was drawn to her, felt a pull like he hadn't experienced in years. It was unsettling, to say the least.

And he needed to figure out why.

"Sooner rather than later, I hope," he whispered to himself.

Chapter Two

Ruth hummed quietly as she walked back to her office. Her most recent session had gone very well—Alex was making great progress with his physical therapy, and Ruth enjoyed being a part of his sessions. By finding and playing the right music for him, she helped him keep on tempo as he learned to walk again. And that wasn't all; she'd heard from several physical therapists that her presence and the music she played for the patients helped them better tolerate some of the more painful exercises.

She flipped through her mental catalog of songs as she walked into the small waiting room outside her office. What should she play for him next time? Alex liked country music, but he'd also mentioned a few rock bands. She unlocked her office door and pushed inside, building a new playlist for their next session. The songs needed to be upbeat, but not too fast…

She sat at her desk and placed her tote bag on a nearby chair. Then she reached for her notebook and a pen and began making a list. Experience had taught her she needed to write these things down or she'd forget as soon as she started thinking about the next patient.

For the next several minutes, Ruth was lost in thought. Her list of songs grew, and she studied each one in turn. She sang softly as she worked her way down the list, checking the tempo, gauging the mood of the music. She also had to consider the lyrics carefully. And there were some songs she'd need to learn how to play herself. Depending on the patient and the session, she could either play the music or use a recording. She generally liked to be prepared for either option.

She played around with the list, changing up the order of the songs until she'd created a solid collection that should help Alex at his next session. Now it was time to search for the music she didn't already know. Moving her list to the side, she looked up to focus on her computer.

That was when she noticed him.

Detective Aguirre was standing in the doorway of her office, his hands in his pockets and one shoulder propped against the jamb as he watched her. When she met his eyes, he offered her a small smile.

"I knocked," he said. "Several times."

"Oh." Ruth felt her cheeks grow warm. "I'm sorry, I didn't notice." It wasn't unusual for her to get lost in her own head when thinking about music. Even as a child, her brain had seemed to shut off to outside stimuli when she was listening to music or playing an instrument. Her family had taken to calling her the absent-minded professor due to her tendency to tune out the world around her.

"How long have you been waiting?"

"Long enough to hear you sing an interesting mash-up of songs." There was a note of amusement in the detective's voice, and Ruth wished her chair would open up and swallow her whole. She had no problem singing for her patients and their families, and she still sang in her church choir. But this was different. She hadn't meant for the detective to hear her sing, and the fact that he'd listened to her felt…personal.

Her dismay must have shown on her face, because his expression switched to apologetic. "I didn't mean to intrude," he said, stepping inside. "And I'm sorry if I made you uncomfortable."

"It's okay," she said, feeling marginally less embarrassed. "I just wasn't expecting you. Do we have an appointment?" She glanced discreetly at her calendar, wondering if she'd managed to forget a meeting. It had only been two days since Lily had shared her story with the detective, and she was scheduled to return to the station to speak with the sketch artist tomorrow. Ruth didn't remember setting up an appointment with the detective, but perhaps she had neglected to write it down?

"We don't," he replied. "I was actually in the neighborhood and thought I'd stop by to touch base with you."

Ruth lifted one eyebrow. "Do you often find yourself wandering an out-of-the-way corridor in the hospital, Detective?"

"Call me Julian," he said. "And today, that's exactly what I found myself doing."

Ruth smiled. Maybe the detective wasn't as stuffy and serious as she'd thought at their first meeting.

"All right, Julian," she said. "I suppose you'd better call me Ruth."

This time, his smile was wide and dazzling. He was handsome before, but with that smile? Irresistible.

"I know you're probably busy," he said. "I was hoping to catch you between clients."

"You did," she replied. "My next session isn't for another half hour. What can I do for you?" She gestured to one of the chairs on the other side of her desk, and he walked over and sat down.

"Have you had a chance to talk to Lily about sharing some of the details of her sessions with me?"

Ruth nodded. She'd been expecting this question, though not the visit. "I have," she said. "Lily has agreed to let me talk to you about our time together. She was going to tell you herself tomorrow, before the meeting with the sketch artist."

"I'd hate to steal her thunder," Julian replied. "I'll pretend not to know."

Ruth tilted her head to the side as she regarded him. "You're good with kids," she remarked. "You made Lily feel very comfortable the other day, which surprised me. She's usually pretty guarded, but she responded well to you."

His brown eyes held hers. "I'm glad to hear it." She heard the genuine sincerity in his voice and knew he meant it.

"I take it you have kids of your own?" It was a personal question, but her curiosity demanded she ask. Once he confirmed his marital status, it would be easier to ignore the growing stirrings of attraction she felt for him.

He dipped his head, looking almost shy. "Uh, no,

actually," he said. "No kids. No wife, either, for that matter. Or girlfriend."

"Oh." Ruth blinked, taking in this new information. So he was single. That was interesting…

"I have a couple of nephews, though," he continued. Was he nervous? He was talking like a man trying to fill the silence, something she sometimes did when she felt uncomfortable. But based on his behavior with Lily the other day, the detective didn't mind lapses in conversation. He'd been quite content to wait while Lily composed her thoughts or got her emotions under control.

"I don't see them as often as I'd like," he said. He met her gaze again, and she saw a flash of vulnerability in his eyes.

"I imagine you work a lot," she said. "It must be hard to find the time."

"That's true." He shrugged. "They live in Texas, so I can't just pop by for a quick visit. But I should make more of an effort." He paused, then leaned forward a bit. "What about you? Do you have kids?"

Ruth saw him glance at her left hand, as though to confirm she still wasn't wearing a ring. She shook her head. "No, no children for me."

"What about nieces or nephews?"

It was an innocent question, one she'd expected. But even though she'd known it was coming, she still felt a pang of sadness at hearing the words. "None of those, either."

She felt his eyes on her, could practically feel his curiosity building. "I'm sorry," he said softly. "I didn't mean to pry."

Ruth took a deep breath and pushed aside her grief.

"It's okay," she said, looking at him once more. "You didn't. My sister died when I was eight years old. She was my only sibling, so unless I marry someone with siblings, I'm never going to be an aunt."

"Oh, man." Julian shook his head. "That's terrible. I'm so sorry for your loss."

"It was a long time ago," Ruth said. But she still carried the pain, and she'd made peace with the fact that she would for the rest of her life. Even though she knew Mary was in heaven, Ruth still felt her loss and mourned her absence.

"Time's a funny thing," Julian said. "Especially when grief is involved. You can feel like you've moved on, and then something will happen and it'll hit you all over again, as strong as ever."

"You've lost someone, too." It wasn't a question. Only someone who was familiar with grief would have that insight.

Julian nodded. "My dad. Several years ago. It was… complicated." He shifted a bit, clearly uncomfortable with the subject.

Ruth offered a small smile. "Family stuff can be hard." It was a lesson she'd learned early on in her work. While she'd been blessed with a close, loving family, not everyone fared the same.

Julian laughed, though there was no humor in it. "You're telling me. Anyway—" he glanced around the room, checking out her space as he changed the subject "—how did you get involved with this?" He gestured to the upright piano against the far wall, and the various drums and tambourines hanging behind her. "Up until a few days ago, I had no idea this career even existed."

"Most people don't." Ruth didn't protest his conversational redirection. She didn't talk about her sister often, especially not with people she'd only just met. But there was something about the detective that made her lower her defenses and had her sharing personal information. He was a good listener, though she knew that was part of his job. The chances of him actually being interested in her sad family history were slim.

Still, she had to admit that his attention felt…nice. She hadn't been on a date in what seemed like forever. The fact that she'd started opening up to a man she barely knew just because he'd asked a few questions and appeared to care about her answers was a sure sign she needed to get out more.

"What is it that you do? What's your typical day look like?"

Ruth shrugged. "That's just it. I don't really have a typical day." She could tell by the expression on his face that the detective wasn't satisfied with her answer, so she continued. "It all depends on my patient schedule. Today, for example, you showed up a few minutes after I had been in a physical therapy session with a patient. This individual is recovering from an accident, and my job is to help keep his spirits up and supplement his physical therapy."

Julian's brows drew together. "How do you do that?"

"With music," she said simply. "I'll play songs on my guitar or ukulele, or sometimes I'll use recordings. The tempo of the songs helps the patient coordinate their movements, and they're also better able to tolerate painful exercises."

"So the music distracts them?"

"It's more than that," Ruth said. "I don't want to bore you with details, but music affects the brain and body in many different ways. It lowers blood pressure, makes pain easier to tolerate and improves mood, just to name a few benefits."

Julian made a noncommittal sound low in his throat.

Ruth could tell he didn't believe her. Normally, she wasn't bothered when people expressed skepticism about what she did for a living. Over the years, she'd heard any number of dismissive responses. People weren't shy about calling her job "hippie nonsense" or even telling her that she was the reason medical costs were so high. Interestingly enough, she never heard those remarks from her actual patients. Only those who had never experienced music therapy discounted its effectiveness.

Maybe she could give the detective a little demonstration… With a few clicks on her computer, she called up a track of rhythmic drumming. She adjusted the volume so they could still talk, then stood and gestured to the sofa on the far side of the wall. "Do you mind if we move to the couch? It's more comfortable."

"Sure." Julian got to his feet and followed her over to it. They sat on opposite ends of the sofa, and Ruth drew her legs up and angled her body to the side to face him.

"You asked me about my day." She reached for one of the small hand drums that sat on the coffee table in front of the sofa and set it on the cushion between them. "I work with patients undergoing physical therapy. I also play for the babies in the hospital nursery a few times a week."

"Sounds like a tough crowd," Julian joked. "Do they even know you're there?"

"Absolutely," Ruth said. "The music settles them and helps them sleep. Sometimes, the nurses will call me if they have to do a painful procedure. They ask me to play because it helps keep the baby calm."

"I'm picking up a theme here," Julian said. "Music as pain relief." He reached for the hand drum and began to examine it, tracing his finger along the surface.

"It's also helpful for patients with dementia," she said. "Many times, people who have forgotten their own children will retain songs from their past. Hearing the music brings them back to life, at least for a few minutes."

"Really?" His fingers began to tap lightly on the drum, keeping time with the rhythm of the track. Ruth hid a smile.

"Yes. Many of my patients have dementia, or mood disorders like depression and anxiety."

"How did Lily Pushkin come to be one of your patients?" Julian held the drum in his lap now, still tapping on the smooth surface without seeming to realize it.

"Her doctor recommended she try music therapy after she started having nightmares. They'd tried a lot of different approaches to help her, but none of them really worked. So they decided on a different tack."

"And does it help?"

Ruth shrugged one shoulder. "You'd have to ask her, but I think so. The nightmares are still there, but they don't seem to happen as often. When she does have one, she's better able to handle it."

Julian nodded, digesting this. "How long have you been working with her?"

"About nine months." Ruth decided it was time she asked some questions of her own. "What about you? How long have you been working this case? Pardon my saying so, but you look too young to have been investigating it from the beginning."

The corner of Julian's mouth lifted in a crooked half smile. "I inherited it, in a way. My first partner after I made detective was named Jim Nelson. He was one of the original detectives assigned to the case. Even after the trail went cold, he stuck with it, trying to find a new angle or lead to pursue."

"When did he die?" she asked quietly.

Julian's fingers stilled on the drum for a few seconds. "Last April." He started drumming again, falling back into the same rhythm.

"You miss him." It wasn't a question. She could tell by Julian's reaction he still mourned the loss of his partner.

"Jim was a good guy," he confirmed. "One of our best. I promised him I wouldn't give up on this case."

Ruth studied his face. There was a tension to the detective's features that went beyond sadness.

He was worried.

She decided to probe a little more. "Are you afraid you won't be able to keep your promise?"

Julian nodded. "Oh, yeah. Every day. When I was working with him, he believed in me. His confidence rubbed off on me and made me feel like I was good at my job, you know?" He shrugged. "Now that he's gone, I'm doubting myself more. Like what if he was propping me up, making me look better than I am?" He trailed off, staring at the drum in his hands. "Wow." He glanced at her, shaking his head. "How did you do that?"

Ruth simply smiled.

A gleam of respect shone in his dark eyes. "So that's how it works."

Ruth tilted her head to the side. "Sort of, yeah. People respond differently, depending on what they need."

Julian shook his head. "How did you do that? I was interrogating you. How did you flip it like that?"

"Interrogating me?" She deliberately kept her tone light, though his choice of words triggered a small wave of discomfort. "And here I thought we were just talking."

A bashful look crossed his face. "Sorry. I didn't mean it like that."

"It's fine," she assured him. Maybe it was inappropriate, but she liked seeing the detective a little flustered. Based on the way he carried himself and his demeanor, she guessed it didn't happen very often.

"To answer your question," she continued, "I didn't manipulate you. At least not deliberately. I gave you something external to focus on. That lowered your defenses and freed up your mind to tell me what you're really thinking."

He lifted the drum he was still holding. "This was a nice touch."

Ruth didn't bother to hide her smile. "Most of my patients like it."

"I might have to ask you to come down to the station the next time I have to interview a suspect." He shook his head, then passed her the drum. "You never did tell me how you got into this field."

Ruth accepted the drum, holding it in her lap. She recognized what the detective was doing—by passing her the instrument, he was asking for her honesty as he rebuilt his walls. For a few seconds, she struggled to decide how she should respond. Should she give him a standard, rote answer? Or tell him the truth, even though it wasn't easy to share?

Let each one of you speak the truth with his neighbor, for we are members of one another... The verse echoed in her head, a reminder from a recent sermon. The pastor had been talking about the importance of honesty and living in truth, even when it was difficult. *Especially* when it was difficult.

Ruth met Julian's eyes, saw the kindness in his gaze. This wasn't part of the case. He wasn't asking because her answer would affect his investigation—he was asking because he was genuinely curious. And after he'd shared some of his truth, she could repay him in kind.

"Mary was my older sister. And she didn't just die," she said. "She was killed after being hit by a drunk driver. We were crossing the street together, and she shoved me out of the way."

Sympathy filled Julian's eyes and he covered her hand with his own. "I'm so sorry."

His touch was warm and comforting, a reassurance that she wasn't alone. "The man who hit her...he was a police officer. He was off duty at the time."

Understanding spread across Julian's face. "Oh no," he said softly.

Ruth nodded. "Despite the evidence, the charges

against him were light. His attorney and union rep argued that he was a stellar officer and that his actions were a one-time aberration. That one mistake shouldn't condemn him for the rest of his life."

"So he got off?" There was a note of disappointed resignation in his voice, as though he already knew the answer.

"Not entirely." Ruth ran her finger along the rim of the drum, pushing down the swell of anger that rose in her chest every time she thought about it. "He was given probation."

"That's hardly justice," Julian remarked. He gave her hand a squeeze and released it. Cool air hit her skin where he'd touched her, sending a shiver of awareness up her arm.

"It was difficult for my family," she said. "We spent a lot of time in church, trying to find forgiveness for him and the system."

Julian was quiet a moment, watching her. "Did you?"

Ruth took a deep breath. "People like to talk as though forgiveness is a one-time deal, something you do once and it's over." She shook her head. "But I've learned it's not that simple. Forgiveness is an ongoing process. A choice you have to make every day. So yes, some days I feel at peace with what happened. Other days…" She trailed off. "Other days are more of a struggle."

Julian stared at her, a strange expression on his face. "I've never thought of it like that before," he said slowly. "But it makes sense."

Ruth smiled. "I'm glad you think so. Anyway, I had a hard time processing what was happening when I was a kid. My parents enrolled me in a music class to give me something else to focus on. It changed my life. When I got older, I realized this field existed, where I could use music to help people. Once I learned about it, I never looked back."

Julian was quiet for a moment. "That's impressive," he said finally. "You took your personal tragedy and turned it into something positive. Most people have a hard time recovering from a loss like that. Fewer still are able to use their pain as inspiration to help others."

"I didn't do it by myself," Ruth replied. The detective's praise made her feel good, but it was important he understood that she wasn't an island. "My family supported me every step of the way. And I have my faith, as well."

"You're saying God helped you?" Julian sounded surprised, as though he hadn't expected her to say that.

Ruth nodded. "Yes." She held her breath, waiting for his reaction. Normally, Ruth didn't talk a lot about her faith. It was personal to her, something she treasured. Sometimes, when she did open up about her beliefs, people dismissed them, calling her naive for believing in a God she couldn't see or touch. Those reactions didn't bother her, because she knew everyone was on their own spiritual journey. But for some reason, she wanted the detective to understand.

He nodded, his expression thoughtful. "Not everyone feels that way." There was something sad about his words that made her wonder.

"What about you?" she asked. "Do you have faith?"

He smiled wryly and shook his head. "Ah, no. I used

to talk to God, but somewhere along the way I felt like no one was listening anymore."

Ruth reached for his hand, an echo of his earlier gesture. "You're not alone," she said, holding his gaze. It was important to her that he realized she was telling the truth. She hated the idea that Julian felt spiritually lonely.

Something flickered in his eyes as he looked at her. Hope, perhaps? She couldn't tell. "I wish I could believe that," he said.

Ruth felt a tug, a pulling force drawing her toward this man. What was it about him that she found so intriguing? He was handsome, yes. There was no doubting that. But her attraction to him went beyond the physical. She wanted to curl up on the sofa and talk to him for hours, to tell him her stories and listen to his. To connect with him and get to know the way his mind worked. Even though she'd spent very little time with him, she felt the beginnings of a connection and wondered where it might lead.

Before she could reply, the sound of voices in the hallway distracted her. Ruth let go of Julian's hand and glanced at her watch, stunned to find it was almost time for her next appointment.

Julian stood and smoothed his hand down the front of his shirt. "I've kept you long enough," he said, smiling apologetically.

Ruth got to her feet, not wanting this visit to end but knowing it must. "Not at all," she said. "It was nice talking to you. We should do it again sometime."

Julian nodded slowly. "I'd like that."

Her heart jumped with anticipation. "I'll see you tomorrow?"

Julian shook his head slightly as though to clear his mind. "Yes. Tomorrow. For the sketch." He sounded a little dazed, and truth be told, she felt that way, too.

"Goodbye, Detective."

"Call me Julian," he reminded her. "Goodbye, Ruth."

He turned and walked through the door, leaving her alone in her office once more. Ruth spun on her heel, her gaze landing on a doll that was sitting on one of the small kid-sized chairs in the corner. "What am I doing?"

Thankfully, the doll made no reply. But Ruth couldn't shake the feeling that something had happened here. She and Julian had shared a moment, one that made her want to spend more time with him. A link was forming between them, at least in her mind. Did he feel the same way? Or did he just see her as a source of assistance in his investigation?

She walked back to her desk and stopped the music. Silence fell over her office, but it didn't stop the voice in her head that whispered, *What if?*

Julian climbed behind the wheel of his truck and sat staring into space. How had that happened? One minute, he was asking Ruth Becker about her job and the work she did, and the next, he was talking about some of his greatest worries and insecurities.

He hardly ever opened up like that. Used to be, he'd talk to Jim when something was on his mind. But since Jim's death, he hadn't had anyone in his life he felt close enough with to share. Certainly not anyone in the department; if he said anything, he'd get labeled as damaged. Things were supposed to be different now, and seeking help no longer had a stigma. But pretty words from administration didn't change the culture overnight, and Julian knew the guys all talked. It was hard enough adjusting to life without his partner and friend. Knowing everyone was whispering behind his back would only make the situation worse.

So what was it about Ruth that had him chattering like a magpie inside of fifteen minutes? He'd been intrigued by her at their first meeting. She had a calm, self-contained composure about her that was appealing. As a detective, Julian often saw people at their worst, when emotions were running high and tempers were short. It was nice to talk to someone who seemed so…stable.

But there was more to it than that. She listened in a way that made him feel heard. He could tell by her expressions that she wasn't simply being quiet until it was her turn to speak again. She seemed to truly care about what he was saying.

"No wonder she's a therapist," he muttered. He would do well to remember that her sympathetic ear was a big part of her job. He shouldn't get too caught up in the fact that a pretty woman seemed interested in his thoughts.

But…their conversation hadn't been all one-sided. She'd shared details from her life, too. Like the story about her sister. Julian shook his head, still frustrated by the lack of justice her family had received. He was all too familiar with the way the force closed ranks to protect their own. As a matter of fact, his father had been a corrupt cop in Phoenix, in with several gangs who had connections to drug cartels. Even as the proof had mounted against him, many of the men he worked with refused to believe what was right in front of their eyes. And worse, some of his fellow officers had "lost" evidence in a bid to help protect his dad. And the sad part was, it had worked. For a time.

Julian ran a hand through his hair, his mind drifting back to the last conversation they'd had. It was just after the grand jury announcement, when his father's indictment had been handed down.

"Why'd you do it?" Julian had asked. He'd been reeling from the realization that his father hadn't been the good guy he'd always thought him to be. Julian had spent his life looking up to his dad, wanting to be like him. He'd joined the police academy to follow in his father's footsteps. But after learning the man wasn't a hero after all, Julian had felt unmoored. He'd always thought his life was built on a foundation of solid rock, but learning the truth about his father had made him realize he was really standing on a pile of shifting sand.

His dad had made excuses, tried to shift the blame onto others. But Julian had cut him off, unwilling to listen. Eventually, his father had given up trying.

"I know I messed up," he'd said. "But do you think you'll ever forgive me for it?"

"No." Julian's response had been swift and sure. His pain had been too great for any other possible answer.

Six hours later, his father was dead.

He'd shot himself with his service revolver, unable or unwilling to accept the consequences of his actions.

At least, that was what Julian thought at the time.

Now, though? He wasn't so sure.

His dad hadn't been perfect. No one was. And while

Julian would never condone his father's actions, he often wondered if it was fair of him to judge the man solely on his mistakes. In that moment, he'd tossed out all the good parts of their relationship, all the childhood moments that had strengthened the bond between them. He'd cast aside his father's love, too hurt to understand how that would affect his dad.

Forgiveness is an ongoing process. A choice you have to make every day.

Ruth's words echoed in his mind. She'd articulated an idea he had gradually discovered for himself. When he'd last spoken to his father, forgiveness had seemed like an abstract concept, something so far out of his reach he couldn't ever imagine finding it. He'd viewed his father's question as a cop-out, an attempt to avoid punishment for his crimes. But now that enough time and distance had passed, Julian recognized that wasn't what his dad had wanted.

If Julian had known then what he knew now—that to forgive didn't mean to forget—would he have responded differently? And if he had, would his father still be alive?

It was a question that haunted him.

Part of him wondered what Ruth would think if she knew. Would she blame him for his dad's actions? For the words he'd said that had seemed to push the other man over the edge? Or would she tell him it wasn't his fault, that his father's actions were his own, and there was nothing Julian could have said or done to change the outcome?

Logically, Julian understood that he himself had not pulled the trigger. But he couldn't help but think that if he hadn't taken away his father's hope of reconciliation, the old man might still be here.

He'd never told anyone about that last conversation. Not even his mother or brother knew what had passed between him and his father. He longed to tell them, to come clean and relieve himself of the guilt he carried. But even though years had gone by, a small part of him was afraid that his family would reject him if they knew what he'd said.

It was ironic, in a way. His words had hurt his father. And he was scared of coming clean, because he knew he wouldn't be able to handle hearing those same words spoken to him by his mother or brother.

Movement caught his eye, and he watched as a younger man helped an older man walk across the hospital parking lot. Father and son? Probably. Julian imagined they were on their way to a doctor's appointment, one generation caring for another.

His heart ached, knowing he would never be able to do that. Sure, his dad had most likely been headed for prison, but Julian still would have been able to visit. It might have taken a while, but Julian liked to think he would have eventually figured out how to move past his father's sins. After all, he certainly wasn't perfect.

Judge not, lest ye be judged.

The quote drifted through his mind, turning his thoughts back to Ruth. In a way, he envied her faith. The way she'd spoken about it made it clear she did take comfort from her beliefs and felt close to God.

What was that like? It had been years since he had prayed. Yeah, he'd gone to church with his family as a kid. But as he'd gotten older, his faith hadn't been able to withstand the slings and arrows of life. Joining the police academy had been a dream come true, but in many ways, it had made him feel even further away from God. His dad's betrayal and subsequent suicide had been the final straw. Julian had abandoned the last vestiges of his faith, certain God had forgotten about him anyway.

Maybe that was why he felt so drawn to Ruth. Even though they hadn't spent much time together, he could tell she was a fundamentally good person. After years of seeing the worst of humanity, it was refreshing to be around someone decent and kind. Someone who wasn't cynical or hard.

No wonder Lily Pushkin responded to her. Julian had opened up to her within twenty minutes. What would he tell her if they spent even more time together?

The thought gave him pause. Thankfully, he hadn't revealed too much to her today. She didn't know about the things he'd said or the way he'd destroyed his relationship with his father. And she didn't need to find out. Julian wanted to see her again, wanted to get to know her better. If she learned the truth about his family situation, she'd want nothing to do with him.

So he wouldn't tell her. He'd been keeping this secret from his mother and brother for years. Why not add one more person to the list?

Julian let out a sigh and started his truck. His day didn't stop simply because a pretty music therapist had thrown him for a loop. There were other cases that needed his attention. Besides, he was going to see her again tomorrow.

For the first time in a long time, anticipation curled

in his belly. It was nice having something to look forward to.

As he pulled out of the parking lot, he couldn't help but wonder: Was his interest one-sided? Or did she feel the same?

Chapter Three

Ruth sat quietly next to Lily as the girl described the features of the man who had been haunting her dreams. She knew this was difficult for Lily—they were asking her to really focus and concentrate on the man who had destroyed her family, when all her protective instincts demanded she think about something, anything else. But Lily was strong and determined. She'd arrived at the police station in a somber mood, but she hadn't hesitated to jump in and start answering questions to help the artist work.

Julian sat on Lily's other side, providing silent support. He hadn't interrupted, hadn't asked Lily any questions of his own. He'd simply greeted her with a smile, a high five and a quietly delivered "I'm proud of you for doing this."

Ruth had seen the look of pleasure cross Lily's face at his words. It was clear she had connected with the detective, and Ruth was glad he had stayed for this meeting. Lily had told her how much she wanted to help Julian catch her parents' killers, and his presence helped Lily feel better as she faced her demons.

Ruth stole a glance at him from the corner of her eyes. After he'd left her office yesterday, she'd had a hard time concentrating. She'd spent the rest of the afternoon wondering about him and wishing they'd had more time to talk. It was nice to be near him again today, even though the circumstances didn't really allow them to chat.

After Lily finished talking to the sketch artist, would Julian need to see them again? He might still have questions about Lily's sessions, but it wouldn't take long for Ruth to fill him in. Was this going to be the last time she had an excuse to talk to him?

The thought made her a little sad. But between one breath and the next, she decided to do something about it. If Julian no longer needed her input for his case, there was no reason Ruth couldn't ask him out to dinner or for a cup of coffee. They'd get another chance to talk, and she could hopefully get over this newfound fascination so she'd be able to focus on her patients again.

The idea of going on a date with Julian made butterflies take flight in her stomach. It had been a while since she'd gone out with a man. Eligible bachelors didn't exactly grow on trees here, and while there were some single men at her church, she'd never felt that spark of interest with any of them. Sometimes, Ruth wondered if she was being too picky. She wanted a husband and kids of her own, but what if God had other plans for her life? Maybe she was supposed to make a difference through her work, rather than by becoming a mother.

It was an issue she'd prayed about, but so far, she'd received no response.

Ruth trusted that God knew what was best for her. But she wasn't willing to give up on her own dreams of a family just yet. This pull she felt toward Julian might turn out to be nothing, but she owed it to herself to at least further investigate. The fact that he was a police officer gave her pause; it was hard to ignore her knee-jerk distrust of cops, based on what had happened with her sister. Still, Julian seemed like a good man, and she wanted to know more about him.

"What do you think?"

Ruth blinked back to attention as the sketch artist turned her notepad around and slid it across the table for Lily's perusal. She studied the image alongside Lily, impressed by the realistic drawing. The face was that of a stranger to her, but Lily appeared to recognize it.

She nodded. "That's him." Her lips pressed together in a thin line of disgust. "That's one of the men who killed my parents."

"Are you sure?" Julian's voice was strained, and Ruth glanced up. He was staring at the drawing, looking as though he'd just seen a ghost.

What's going on? she wondered. Unless she missed her guess, Julian recognized this guy. But how was that possible?

A hurt look flashed across Lily's face. "I'm pretty sure," she said.

Julian turned to her and smiled apologetically. "Of course you are," he said. "I don't doubt your memory. But I have a question for you—did this man kill your parents, or did he watch while the other man acted?"

Ruth frowned at the leading question. Julian appeared to hold his breath as he waited for Lily to respond, making it seem like he was hoping for a certain answer.

"I…I'm not certain," Lily said. Doubt shadowed her face and she seemed to shrink in the chair.

"Think, please," Julian urged. He glanced up and Ruth lifted one brow in warning. Julian had been careful not to pressure Lily during their first interview, and because he'd made her feel safe, Lily had agreed to meet today. Ruth wasn't about to let him bully her, no matter how eager he was to solve the case.

"I'm sorry, Lily," Julian said. He placed his hand between her shoulder blades and softened his voice. "You've done a great job here today. I appreciate you talking to me again and describing this man to the sketch artist."

Lily nodded. "I'll try to remember more details," she said. "It's hard, though, 'cause the other man had his back to me most of the time."

"You've helped me so much already," Julian assured her. "I don't want you to stress about remembering more."

Ruth softened a bit at his words, and she noticed some of the tension left Lily's shoulders, too.

"Okay," the girl said. "Can I go now?"

"Of course," Julian replied. He helped her slide back the heavy chair so she could stand. Lily gave a shy smile to the sketch artist, who was packing up her supplies.

"I want you to know you can call me if there's ever anything I can do to help you," Julian said to Lily. Ruth followed them to the door, hanging back a bit so as not to interrupt.

"I will," Lily said. "I hope I can remember more stuff for you."

"It's all right if you don't," Julian said. "I want you to focus on school and your friends and having fun. Let me worry about everything else."

Lily smiled as he opened the door. "I'll try."

Julian gave her grandparents a little wave as Lily walked out to greet them. Before Ruth could leave, the sketch artist stepped forward and exchanged a few quiet words with Julian as she handed him the sketch. He nodded and looked at the image again as the woman left. One hand came up to rub the back of his neck as he studied the likeness. Once again, Ruth couldn't help but think Julian knew more about this man than he was letting on.

She took a step forward, intending to sneak past him while he was still distracted by the sketch. But she wasn't as stealthy as she'd hoped, because he glanced up as soon as she started to move.

"Hey," he said, rolling the paper into a tube so the image was no longer visible. "I've been thinking since our talk yesterday, and…" He trailed off, a slight flush appearing on his cheeks.

He's nervous, she realized with a small shock. What was going on here?

Julian met her eyes as he took a breath. "Would you like to grab dinner with me?"

Ruth felt her jaw drop as happiness bloomed in her chest. He *was* interested in her! She felt a smile start to spread over her face and fought to control it so she wouldn't seem alarmingly eager.

"Yes," she managed, nodding. "That would be nice."

Some of the tension lines around Julian's eyes relaxed. "Great. Are you free tomorrow?"

Friday night. Dinner with a handsome, interesting man. Ruth hadn't expected such a surprising development when she'd started her day, but she wasn't about to complain. "I am. What did you have in mind?"

"Do you like Mexican food?"

Ruth nodded, pleased with the direction he was going.

"There's a place called Tia Maria's on the edge of town. The neighborhood is a little rough, but the food is amazing."

"I've heard of it." The paper had done a story about the owner a few months ago, and she'd made a mental note to try it sometime. But between work and choir rehearsals, she hadn't been able to meet up with any of her friends for a girls' night in a while. Going with Julian was an even better option.

"Can I pick you up?" he asked. "Like I said, the area isn't the greatest. We get a lot of calls about stolen cars and property damage on the weekends. I'd hate for you to have any trouble like that."

Ruth nodded, appreciating his offer. "That's fine." Normally, she insisted on meeting a date rather than letting him pick her up. But based on their interactions so far, she knew Julian was a good guy and she was starting to trust him.

He handed over his cell phone. "Will you add your number? I could pull it off of my desk phone, but this will be faster," he said. "I'll can text you for your address later."

Ruth typed in the digits, part of her still marveling that this moment was actually happening. Maybe she wasn't as out of practice as she'd thought…

She handed him his phone and he smiled. Anticipation flared to life in her chest, and she wondered how she was going to be able to concentrate at work tomorrow, knowing she would be seeing Julian again so soon.

"I'll text you later," he said, holding the door open for her. "There's a few things I need to take care of first." A shadow crossed his face, reminding Ruth of his earlier reaction to seeing the completed sketch. Curiosity urged her to ask him about it, but the practical voice in her head told her to wait. Hopefully Lily's description would provide a break in the case. But why, then, had Julian seemed so shaken by the image? That part didn't add up, and Ruth wanted to know more.

She smiled at him, deciding to bide her time. They'd talk at dinner tomorrow. She could ask him about the case then.

Their date couldn't come soon enough.

Julian watched Ruth walk away, wishing he could go after her. He'd taken a risk asking her to dinner, and he was glad she'd accepted his invitation. If he had his way, he'd skip straight to their date tomorrow so he could spend more time with her. But it wasn't that easy. First, he had to respond to this new development in the case.

He walked back to his desk, tapping the rolled-up sketch against his thigh as he moved. Nervous energy thrummed through Julian's body, making him feel unsettled. He sat, and after a quick glance around to make sure no one was paying attention to him, he unrolled the sketch on his desk.

Recognition hit him once more, an unpleasant shock that made his stomach churn. The image hadn't changed—he'd known it wouldn't. But a small part of him had hoped that maybe he'd made a mistake. Maybe he was simply looking at the drawing from the wrong angle, seeing something that wasn't really there.

Now, though, as he stared at the likeness, Julian was forced to admit he hadn't been wrong. He *did* know this man.

Sam Watkins.

He knew him from the police academy. Julian had just started as Sam was leaving, but they'd spoken a time or two and Sam had been generally helpful. But while Julian had left Phoenix, hoping to make a fresh start away from his father's tarnished reputation, Sam had found a job with the Phoenix PD. They'd kept in touch a bit after Julian's graduation, and Julian knew Sam had started to make a name for himself in the Phoenix gang unit, even doing some undercover work.

So why had he been at the Pushkins' house that fateful night?

Julian shook his head, trying to make sense of it. The Sam he'd known would never have committed murder. Surely the man hadn't fundamentally changed that much in the intervening years?

But what if…what if he hadn't been there at all? Maybe Lily's memories were fuzzy, leading her to describe someone that resembled Sam but wasn't actually him. It was possible the sketch artist hadn't gotten the likeness exactly right, and in fact the true suspect wasn't Sam at all. Didn't everyone have a double out there somewhere?

Even as hope flared to life in his chest, Julian knew it was an unlikely possibility. Lily had never seen Sam before. Neither had the sketch artist. What were the odds that Lily's description and the sketch artist's work would result in an image that just happened to look very much like Sam? Sure, it wasn't a perfect rendering, but it was close enough that Julian had recognized him even though he hadn't seen the man in years. No, the simplest, most plausible explanation was that Sam had been at the Pushkin house that night, and Lily had seen his face.

Had he been the one to pull the trigger and end her parents' lives? A wave of revulsion washed over Julian at the thought. Hopefully his old friend hadn't been the one to kill the Pushkins. But…if Sam had stood back and done nothing while the other intruder committed murder, was that truly any better?

Whatever the outcome, Julian had to pursue this. He couldn't simply pretend like he didn't know about Sam's involvement in the Pushkin murder case. But he had to be careful. If Sam was still undercover, he couldn't just call him up and start asking questions. He'd have to go through the proper channels to talk to him. Depending on Sam's current assignment, he likely had a designated check-in appointment with someone in his department. Julian would have to leave a message asking Sam to contact him.

And that was where things could stall. If the department contact didn't like what Julian had to say, or if Sam's current assignment was too sensitive for any outside contact, Sam might not get back to him for days, possibly even weeks or months. Julian had to be careful here; he had to stress his need to talk to Sam without giving away the reasons.

With a sigh, he pulled up a roster of contacts from the Phoenix PD. He'd start with a few targeted calls, and if that didn't work, he'd have to bring his supervisor on board. Hopefully, it wouldn't come to that point. If word got around that an officer was suspected of involvement in the Pushkin case, it would make his job infinitely more complicated. He was definitely going to have to tread carefully here.

He just hoped it would pay off.

Chapter Four

Ruth couldn't remember the last time she'd enjoyed a meal this much. The food was delicious, the ambience great. But it was the man across from her who really made it enjoyable.

They'd talked nonstop since he'd picked her up, about anything and everything. They'd chatted about their families, their friends, favorite movies and books. All the typical getting-to-know-you topics. Now they'd moved on to random stories. At the moment, Julian was laughing as she told him about the surprising way her cat, Morris, had appeared in her life.

His laughter was low and sonorous and deeply appealing. Like his smile, the sound softened his image, making him seem more approachable.

Something told Ruth that Julian didn't have a reason to laugh very often. But it was clear he was enjoying himself tonight. And the soft, feminine part of her felt emboldened by the fact that she was causing this hard, serious man to relax.

"So he just strolled in like he owned the place?"

"Pretty much," she confirmed. "I had never seen this cat before in my life until the day he appeared out of thin air."

"I'm trying to imagine that first encounter," Julian said. His brown eyes shone with amusement. "How did that go, exactly?"

"It wasn't my finest moment," Ruth said. She took a sip of tea and continued. "I wasn't expecting a cat at all, so when I woke up that morning and found him lying on my new couch, I screamed a bit. He opened one eye to glare at me and then went back to sleep." She shook her head, recalling Morris's indignant expression at her daring to interrupt his sleep.

"So what did you do?" Julian scooped some salsa onto a chip and took a bite as he waited for her response.

"I called the furniture company and asked if he belonged to one of the delivery guys. They said no and acted like I was a little odd to even be asking the question. I guess this had never happened before?"

"Probably not a regular thing," Julian said.

"So then I started knocking on my neighbors' doors," Ruth continued. "I figured one of them had accidentally let their cat out and they were missing him. But no one claimed him. I wound up taking him to the vet and he didn't have a chip. That's when I knew I had to accept my fate."

"Sounds like he chose you."

Ruth nodded. "He did. I guess he wandered inside while the door was open and managed to hide during all the activity. Once things calmed down, he must have felt safe enough to come out and lay claim to his new digs."

"It was good of you to keep him," Julian said. "Not

everyone would be so willing to tolerate a new room-mate who showed up unannounced."

Ruth smiled. "The timing of it was interesting. I'd been thinking about getting a cat anyway. I figured I'd go to the local shelter, but then Morris turned up and now here we are."

Julian raised his water glass and tipped it in a mock toast. "I guess it was meant to be."

"You know what they say," Ruth remarked as she dipped a chip into the shared salsa. "God works in mysterious ways."

"No kidding," Julian replied.

"What about you?" she asked. "Have you had any random animals show up at your place?"

"I'm afraid not," Julian said. "I get the odd cock-roach, but I definitely don't encourage them to stick around."

Ruth wrinkled her nose. "Definitely not."

"I'd really like to get a dog," he continued. "But I don't think I'm home enough. It wouldn't be fair for me to leave them home alone all day."

"Cats are much better with solitude," Ruth said.

"That's what I've heard, but I haven't done much research into cats as pets."

She studied him over the rim of her iced tea glass. "You need to research pet cats?" An image of Julian hunched over a computer poring through an internet forum on cats sprang to mind, and she suppressed a smile.

"Well, yeah." His tone made it clear that he found the idea obvious. "I mean, you have to know what to feed them, what kind of litter they need, what kind of toys they like." He shrugged. "It's a lot."

"I see." She nodded thoughtfully, biting her lip. "I've found it's mostly a trial-and-error process when it comes to toys. As for food, Morris isn't picky. And cat litter is pretty much all the same, no matter what brand."

"That's good to know."

Their conversation paused as the waiter delivered their food. It looked good and smelled even better.

Things were going well so far. Maybe a little too well? Julian seemed like a great guy. But was she over-looking a flaw because he'd connected well with Lily? She was glad he'd made Lily feel comfortable, but that didn't mean she should give him the benefit of the doubt in all things. She knew better than most people that not all police officers were heroes; she had to make sure Julian was truly a good man before she fully trusted him.

"I'm glad you suggested this place," she told him as they both started to eat.

"It's one of my favorites," he replied as he cut into his enchiladas. "Jim brought me here several years ago. I don't eat here as often as I'd like, so I was glad you agreed to join me."

She smiled as they started eating. Even though their conversation had flowed effortlessly and she was en-joying getting to know Julian better, she was still cu-rious about his reaction to seeing the finished sketch yesterday. His response didn't sit well with her, and she needed an explanation. But how could she bring it up without ruining the mood?

"You like to have all the i's dotted and t's crossed before you do anything, don't you?" she asked.

Julian nodded. "It's good to be careful."

"Probably comes in handy with your job."

"It does," he said. "I like to be thorough. It's important I don't overlook any details in my work. Sometimes it's the little things that help me solve a case."

"What about Lily's case?" she asked. This was an opening she could use. "She's told you a lot about her memories. Has any of that helped?"

Julian tilted his head to the side as he considered her question. "In many ways, yeah. There's no smoking gun, so to speak, but some of the details she's talked about are helping me see the evidence with fresh eyes."

"And the sketch?" Ruth tried to keep her tone casual, but she watched Julian's expression carefully to see if he'd react.

He paused. Not for very long—maybe half a second—but she caught the subtle tightening of his lips before he replied.

"We haven't released it to the public yet," he said, taking a sip of his drink. "There are a few things I'm looking into before we do that."

"Like what?" She took another bite, hoping he didn't read too much into her interest.

He narrowed his eyes slightly. "Just some i's to dot and t's to cross," he said. "You seem awfully interested in what's going to happen with the sketch."

Ruth shrugged. "I just want Lily to find some closure." *And I want to know why you looked like you'd seen a ghost.* Was that a sign she couldn't trust him?

Julian nodded. "I do, too. I'm hoping I can solve this once and for all. For her and for Jim."

The conversation shifted to lighter topics, and soon

they were laughing together again. Julian offered to pay for her meal, and Ruth agreed.

"Thank you again," she said as they started walking down the street. The small parking lot of the restaurant had been full when they'd arrived, so Julian had been forced to park his truck on a narrow side street. Ruth hadn't thought twice about it at the time, but now that it was dark, she appreciated his presence. There weren't many working streetlamps in this area, and the surroundings that had looked derelict in the light now appeared downright sinister.

"My pleasure," Julian said. "This has been really nice. Maybe we can do it again sometime?"

Ruth smiled and was about to reply when a movement caught her eye. A shadow detached itself from a fence and began to approach. There was something about the way this person moved that made the hairs on the back of her neck stand on end, and she grabbed Julian's arm.

Julian immediately stepped in front of her, using his body to shield her from this unknown and unexpected presence. Ruth's heart pounded in her chest and her mind raced—were they about to get mugged?

"Hey," Julian said cautiously. Did he know this person? Or was he just offering a greeting to defuse the tension of the moment?

Ruth soon got her answer. "Heard you're looking for me." It was a man's voice attached to the shadow. As soon as Julian heard it, he relaxed. *He knows this guy*, she realized.

She peeked around Julian's body to see who was speaking. Shock washed over her in a cold wave, freezing her in place and turning her meal to a stone in her stomach. "You're the one in the sketch!" she gasped.

The man glanced at her, then back to Julian. "What sketch?" he demanded. "What's she talking about?"

Julian clenched his jaw. "Give me a minute, okay?" he said to the man. He turned to Ruth. "I need you to wait in my truck, please."

Ruth stared up at him, confusion making it hard for her to think. "Julian, what is going on here? That's the man Lily described." She kept her voice low, hoping he wouldn't hear her. "Aren't you going to arrest him?"

Julian's expression made him look like a stranger. Gone was the friendly, easygoing man she'd just had dinner with. In his place was a hard, cold, unreadable man. "No," he said shortly. "Please wait in my truck." He tugged on her arm, pulling her toward the passenger side of his vehicle.

Ruth was too surprised to protest. Julian unlocked the door and unceremoniously boosted her into the seat. "Sit tight," he ordered. Then he shut the door and clicked the locks into place with his key fob.

Ruth watched him walk back to the man, her initial shock quickly giving way to anger. She knew she wasn't seeing things—that was the same man Lily had described as being at her home the night of her parents' murder. And while the girl hadn't been able to tell Julian if this guy had pulled the trigger, the fact that he'd been there was still incriminating. He could lead them to the other man, so why wasn't Julian arresting him?

Because they're connected. She could tell by Julian's body language that he knew this man. And while she didn't think Julian himself had anything to do with the

Pushkins' deaths, he did have some kind of relationship with this stranger. No wonder he'd been so spooked by seeing the sketch.

Maybe she'd been wrong to trust him after all. It was clear he wasn't being fully open about his approach to Lily's case. Given this new turn, Ruth was glad he hadn't mentioned any plans to speak to Lily again.

She kept her attention on Julian. Were they friends? She studied the man as he and Julian spoke. They were about the same age. Maybe childhood pals? Not brothers; there was no resemblance between them. But as she watched, another figure approached on the sidewalk. Both the stranger and Julian fell into identical stances as the new person passed by. Ruth watched the two of them move, disbelief building in her chest and tears stinging her eyes as awareness dawned.

Whoever he was, this man wasn't just Julian's friend.

He was also a cop.

And she knew all too well that cops protected their own.

Disgust filled her, making her stomach churn. So much for trusting her instincts. Ruth could have sworn that Julian was different. That he wasn't like the men who had minimized her sister's death to keep their buddy out of jail. No, Julian had seemed like one of the good guys.

But now she saw the truth.

He was choosing his friend's freedom over justice for Lily. It was that simple.

And that heartbreaking.

There would be time later, she knew, to reexamine their interactions and try to figure out how she'd so spectacularly misjudged Julian. What signs she'd missed, what little tells she'd overlooked thanks to her attraction to him. But she couldn't focus on herself now. She was determined to push aside her own hurt and focus on Lily. She wasn't about to let the system harm another little girl, not when she had the power to do something about it.

Ruth pulled her phone from her purse and clicked on the rideshare app. She quickly typed in her information and was rewarded a few seconds later with an update that her ride would be here in two minutes.

Good, she thought. Then she snuck a quick picture of Julian and his friend, trying to focus on the man's face. It was a little blurry thanks to the low light, but it would have to do.

Julian and his friend seemed to be wrapping up their conversation just as Ruth spotted her ride. The other man walked away and Julian made it to the driver's-side door before she hopped out and flagged the car down.

"Ruth, what are you doing?"

She heard the confusion in his tone but didn't look back. "I'm leaving," she said.

She picked up the pace, but Julian was faster than she'd anticipated. His hand wrapped around her arm, stopping her.

Ruth turned and glared at him, her heart pounding hard. If he wanted to, he could force her back into the truck. She was no match for him physically.

He released her immediately and held up his hands. "I know that looked bad," he started.

"Bad?" she repeated. "You think? You're letting him go because he's your friend!"

"That's not true," he said, but she cut him off.

"You said you cared about Lily, but you don't."

Julian's eyes flashed with emotion. "You don't understand," he said. "He's not just my friend."

"I know," Ruth replied tightly. "He's a cop."

Julian reeled back as though she'd struck him. His reaction confirmed her suspicion, renewing her anger. "How did you know that?"

Ruth shook her head. "It doesn't matter. I know how you are. I thought you were different, but I guess I was wrong. You guys are all the same. You protect each other, no matter the cost to the innocent people who get in the way." Her voice shook, but not from sadness. No, it was fury that tightened her throat and made it difficult to speak.

Awareness spread over Julian's face as he made the connection. "No, Ruth, it's not like that."

"Spare me," she said. "I'm leaving." She started walking to the waiting car again.

"Ruth, please!" Julian called after her. "I can explain."

Ruth ignored him as she climbed into the car. Part of her wanted to hear him out, to listen to what he had to say. But she knew it wouldn't matter. Julian had shown her who he really was. She owed it to herself, and to Lily, to heed his actions rather than his pretty words.

She blinked back tears as the driver pulled onto the main road. Her stomach churned with emotion, and for a brief, panicky moment, she realized she didn't know what to do next. Where was she supposed to go for help when the police officer working this case was corrupt? Who was going to solve Lily's case now?

"I'll figure something out," she muttered to herself. She sent up a silent prayer, asking for strength and guidance. There had to be a solution to this problem.

And she *would* find it.

Julian waited until nine on Saturday morning to call her. Ruth was already upset with him; he didn't want to wake her up and give her another reason to be angry.

He wasn't surprised when she didn't answer the phone. He debated hanging up without leaving a message, but decided he had to at least try to reach her.

"Ruth, I need to talk to you. I want to tell you what happened last night. I know things looked bad, but please believe me when I say there's an explanation for everything you saw."

He hung up and rubbed the back of his neck, his eyes gritty with fatigue.

Julian hadn't slept last night. Sam's surprise arrival had thrown him for a loop, and then after Ruth had stormed off... His stomach churned at the memory of her face, the look of betrayal she'd given him just before hopping into the car she'd called to pick her up.

Not that he blamed her. He hadn't exactly been transparent about what was going on, and why he was talking to the man Lily had described to the sketch artist. If he didn't have all the facts, he probably would have jumped to the very same conclusions she'd drawn. Part of him admired her for taking matters into her own hands and leaving without a backward glance. Ruth might be quiet, but she definitely wasn't passive.

Still, he couldn't deny that her reaction had hurt his feelings. They'd had such a good time at dinner—why hadn't she at least given him the chance to explain last night? This whole misunderstanding could have been avoided if she'd only listened for a few minutes instead of running away.

Now that some time had elapsed, he hoped her temper had cooled enough to hear him out. Their dinner had gone so well last night, and he'd truly enjoyed talking to her and getting to know her better. For the first time in a long time, he felt a connection to a woman and he wanted to find out where it would lead. He'd dated some in the past, but never really felt a spark. He'd always prioritized his work over relationships, so it was no surprise those relationships never lasted long.

But he felt different with Ruth. To his surprise, the pull he felt toward her nearly outweighed the pull he felt to his job. Julian had a suspicion that if he spent more time with Ruth, he'd eventually grow to put her above his work. It was a thought that he found both appealing and scary at the same time.

He sighed. Unless she was willing to talk to him, his feelings weren't going to matter. The idea that their relationship might be over before it even really got started was enough to darken his mood, but he wasn't going to push her. He'd call her one more time, and if she didn't respond to his messages, he'd take the hint.

And as for the investigation? That was one thing he wasn't going to give up on. No matter what Ruth thought of him, he wasn't like the cops who had protected her sister's killer. After talking to Sam last night, Julian was more convinced than ever that the Pushkin case wasn't a straightforward home invasion gone wrong. Something deeper was going on here. Jim had always suspected it, but he'd never been able to prove his hunches. Julian, however, had a huge advantage—Lily. Her memories were going to be the key to breaking this case wide open. He just had to figure out how all the pieces fit together.

Feeling jittery, he checked his phone again. Only a few minutes had elapsed since he'd called Ruth, but he couldn't wait any longer. He needed to resolve this issue, for better or worse.

He dialed her number again and held his breath. *Please, please, please*, he repeated silently. He wasn't sure who he was talking to—God? He hadn't prayed in years. Would this even count?

Before he could wonder too much about what constituted a prayer, Ruth answered the phone.

"Hello?" Her tone was guarded, almost reluctant. It was clear she didn't want to talk to him, but she was doing it anyway.

Thanks, Julian thought, sending a bit of gratitude out into the universe. This was going to be his only shot. He had to take advantage of it.

"Ruth, it's Julian," he said. "Thank you for answering my call."

She hesitated for a few seconds, and he feared she might hang up. "What do you want, Julian?"

He took a deep breath. "I'd like to talk about what happened last night. I know things looked bad, but I want to explain."

"I saw what happened," she replied, her voice taking on an edge. "The man Lily described as being in her home when her parents were killed walked over to us and you started talking to him like you're old friends."

Julian bit his tongue to keep from going on the defensive. Her lack of trust in him stung, but he couldn't let it affect his tone. "Yes, that is true. I did that."

He could sense Ruth's surprise through the connection. "Why?" she asked after a moment. There was a lot of emotion in that one word: anger, hurt, fear. Julian realized anew how his actions must have made Ruth think the worst of him. He wished he could go back in time and change his response to seeing Sam, but all he could do was move forward and hope Ruth would give him another chance.

"I know you don't want to talk to me, and I know I made mistakes last night," he said. "But there is an explanation for everything you saw. Will you meet me in an hour so I can talk to you in person?"

When she didn't reply right away, he continued. "There's a coffee shop by the bookstore on Green Valley Street. They make really good apple fritters. Can we meet there to talk? If you don't like what I have to say, you can leave and I promise I won't bother you again. But I would appreciate the chance to clarify what happened last night and share with you how it's going to affect my investigation."

He held his breath as he waited for her response. Ruth was a reasonable person. Would she give him another chance?

"All right," she said. "One hour."

He exhaled softly. "Thanks, Ruth."

"Don't thank me yet," she warned. "I might not like what you have to say."

"I'm just grateful you're willing to listen." It was the truth. At least she was going to hear him out. If she decided to walk away after he'd said his piece, at least he'd know he'd tried everything to make this right.

They ended the call and he shot to his feet. There were some things he needed to take care of before meeting Ruth, and an hour didn't give him much time.

But he would get it done. He had no other choice.

Chapter Five

Ruth stepped inside the coffee shop and glanced cautiously around. She didn't see Julian, but then again, she was a little early.

She ordered a hot tea and claimed a small table near the window. The warm scent of fresh-baked goods filled the air, but she was too tense to eat anything. Her throat felt so tight that just swallowing her tea was trial enough.

For the millionth time, she asked herself what she was doing here. Why was she giving Julian another chance? His actions last night had been clear. What could he possibly say that would make her excuse his behavior?

When she'd woken this morning, she'd wondered if maybe she'd made a mistake. The darkness last night meant she hadn't gotten a perfectly clear view of the man's face. Perhaps she was mistaken, and he wasn't really the same man Lily had described to the sketch artist?

But her doubts had been dispelled when Julian had

confirmed her suspicions over the phone. She'd accused him of talking to the man like an old friend, and he'd admitted it. Case closed.

And yet, here she was, waiting for Julian to arrive and tell her his side of the story. As if this was a situation where knowing the other side mattered.

Was she a sucker for coming? Was she setting herself up to be lied to, to be made to doubt what she'd seen with her own eyes? She'd experienced gaslighting before, after her sister's death. As a child herself, she'd been ill-equipped to handle it. But she was a grown woman now. And she wasn't about to let another police officer try to convince her that things weren't as bad as they seemed.

Most importantly, though, was she betraying Lily? She'd made no promises to believe what Julian told her, but was her willingness to even listen going to wind up hurting Lily? The thought was too disturbing to dwell on for long.

Despite all her misgivings, a small, naive part of Ruth's heart hoped this was all a big misunderstanding. The Julian she was getting to know seemed like a decent, honorable man. The stories he'd shared with her about some of his cases, the way he talked about his old partner, Jim, and the things he'd told her about his mother and brother…he appeared to be a truly good guy. Maybe last night was a blip, an uncharacteristic mistake on his part that he was trying to correct. Didn't she at least owe him a chance to explain?

Ruth couldn't deny that she wanted to give him the benefit of the doubt. It hurt to think she'd so badly misjudged him, and her attraction to him hadn't disappeared overnight. A selfish voice whispered in her ear to give him another chance. She didn't want to say goodbye to him yet, but she might not have a choice.

Her mind circled back to Lily. In truth, Ruth had agreed to meet Julian for Lily's sake as well as her own. She needed to know what Julian was planning on doing with respect to the Pushkin investigation. Lily deserved both answers and justice. If Julian wasn't going to pursue either, Ruth had some decisions to make.

The bell over the door chimed and Ruth looked up to see Julian walk in. Her stomach did a little flip at the sight of him, her body unaffected by her current emotional state.

He looked over and saw her, an expression of relief sweeping across his features.

He didn't think I'd come, she realized.

Julian gestured to the counter and she nodded. A few minutes later he joined her at the table, coffee in hand.

"Sorry about the delay," he said. "I need the caffeine."

She studied his face as he placed a manila file folder on the table between them. There were dark circles under his eyes, and his cheeks sported a dusting of stubble. His shirt was clean but slightly wrinkled, as though he'd grabbed the first thing he'd found when getting dressed. It was a far cry from his usual polished look, and Ruth got the impression he hadn't slept much last night.

Well, that made two of them.

"Thank you for meeting me," he said. "Before we get started, I talked to my boss and he's agreed to make you a consultant on the Pushkin case."

Ruth frowned. "What does that mean?"

Julian tapped the folder with his forefinger. "It means I can share all the details of the case with you. You can be a part of every step in my investigation. If you want to be, that is."

"Okay." She drew the word out, uncertain how to respond. What did it mean to be a consultant on a case? And why was Julian doing this?

Her confusion must have shown on her face, because he continued. "I did this because I want you to know I'm being totally honest and transparent with you. There were things I couldn't talk to you about before. Now I can."

Ruth felt her curiosity build. "Like what?"

"Like the man last night," Julian said. "You're right—I do know him. His name is Sam Watkins. We overlapped a bit at the police academy. He stayed on in Phoenix while I moved here. Last I heard, he was part of the gang unit doing undercover work."

Ruth pressed her lips together but didn't interrupt.

"As soon as I saw the sketch, I reached out to my contacts with a message that I needed to talk to Sam. Like I said, he's infiltrated the Rising Suns gang, so I can't just call him up for a chat. I never expected him to find me, and certainly not so soon after I asked about him."

"Was he there the night Lily's parents were killed?"

Julian shook his head. "He says he wasn't. He said six years ago, when he was working on getting initiated into the gang, there was another recruit who looked a lot like him. That the guys used to tease them about being brothers. He thinks that the other man might be the person Lily remembers seeing."

Ruth tilted her head to the side. It sounded like a flimsy excuse to her, but she had to know what Julian thought. "Do you believe him?"

"I don't know yet," he replied. "Sam helped me a bit before he graduated, and he seemed like a decent guy. But I've misjudged people before." A faraway look entered his eyes and then he shook his head slightly. "What I do know is that this gang has a reputation for violence, and they aren't picky. They've been known to take jobs from people who don't want to get their hands dirty. It's possible if this other guy exists, he was sent to the Pushkins' house with a veteran member as part of his initiation."

"Initiation?" Ruth repeated. "What does that mean?"

Julian's face went carefully blank, and she got the impression she didn't want to know details. "People who want to join a gang are often asked to participate in illegal activities to prove their loyalty," he said. "The more violent the gang, the more violent the crime they're asked to commit."

"Oh." She took a sip of her tea, connecting the dots. "So you think this recruit was asked to kill the Pushkins to earn his spot?"

Julian shrugged. "It's possible. But Lily said she saw two men in the house that night, which is consistent with some of the forensic evidence. So it's possible the other guy pulled the trigger by himself, or they both participated."

"Either way, your friend says he wasn't there?"

"That's correct." Julian took a sip of his coffee. "I'm not going to lie to you, Ruth. I want to believe him. But it's been years since we've really talked, and given his assignment…well, the stuff I'm sure he's seen can change a man." He ran a hand through his hair. "I don't know what to think right now."

Ruth swallowed and asked the question that had been plaguing her since last night. "Are you trying to protect him?"

Julian's eyes went wide. "No!" he exclaimed. He leaned forward and covered her hand with his. "Not in the way you think," he amended, lowering his voice. "If it turns out Sam is involved in this case, I won't hesitate to arrest him. But if he's not part of it and I move too quickly, the gang could turn on him. You don't want to know what they do to people who betray them." He shuddered, and a chill went down Ruth's spine. "If Sam is innocent and I mess this up, I'd be signing his death warrant."

"That's why you didn't do anything last night," she said, seeing the events with a fresh perspective.

"Exactly," Julian confirmed. "The fact is, I don't have enough evidence to make a move."

"What about the sketch?" Ruth asked. "Doesn't that count for something?" Indignation rose in her chest on Lily's behalf. Why ask the girl to relive her trauma if it wasn't useful for the investigation?

"Oh, the sketch helps, don't get me wrong," Julian assured her. "But it's circumstantial, at best. The sketch alone won't hold up in court. Eyewitnesses are notoriously unreliable, and any defense attorney worth their salt will argue that the six-year-old memories of a traumatized child—a girl of just four—aren't to be trusted."

"What about you?" she asked quietly. "Do you believe her?" It was the second time she'd asked him that question, but his answer would help her decide what to do next. Her anger toward him had faded in light of the new information he'd shared with her, but she was still concerned about the investigation. Mostly, though, she worried about Lily and how this was going to affect the girl.

Julian met her gaze, sincerity shining in his eyes. "I do believe her, yes. And I wish that was enough. But I need more."

Ruth let out the breath she didn't realize she'd been holding. "It's okay. As long as you're on Lily's side, I'll do whatever I can to help you."

Julian smiled at her. Some of the tension seemed to leave his shoulders. "Thank you," he said simply.

She watched him take another sip of his coffee and realized it was her turn to be transparent. "I'm sorry," she said.

He blinked at her over the rim of his cup. "Um, what?"

"I'm sorry," she repeated. "I rushed to judgment last night, and I didn't give you a chance to explain. I disregarded everything I knew about you and jumped to the conclusion you were doing something shady. I should have listened to you. I should have trusted you a little more." She glanced down, feeling embarrassed. While she was relieved to know the truth, part of her felt bad for having so misjudged Julian. She wouldn't blame him if he wanted to keep things professional from now on—she certainly wouldn't want to have a relationship with someone who didn't trust her, or who immediately thought the worst when something happened.

"Hey." He leaned forward, waiting for her to meet his eyes. When she did, all she saw was understanding. "I don't blame you and I'm not upset with you. I mean, I was a little irritated, but I get it. What you did last night was smart—you felt like you were in a dangerous situation, and you bailed as safely as possible. I wasn't forthcoming with information, and you put two and two together and came up with four. Any reasonable person would have done the same. And after what you've told me about your sister and her case…" He trailed off, shaking his head. "It's no wonder you were suspicious when you realized Sam was a cop and I wasn't going to arrest him."

"I'm glad you called me today," she said softly.

"I'm glad you picked up," he replied.

"I almost didn't," she admitted.

"I guess God decided to answer my prayer today," he said dryly.

A frisson of shock traveled through her limbs. "You prayed about this?" She couldn't hide the surprise in her voice. Julian had said the other day his faith was battered. Was he starting to rebuild it?

He shrugged, looking suddenly bashful. "I don't know. I mean, maybe that's what I did? It wasn't anything formal, that's for sure. It probably doesn't even count as a prayer."

Ruth smiled, pleased to hear he was even thinking about the subject. "Prayer comes from the heart. That's all it takes."

"Then…I guess I did pray." He sounded a little surprised, as though he couldn't quite believe he'd done it.

"How did it feel?" Ruth asked.

"I'm not sure," he said. "I'm still trying to figure that out."

"Join the club." She lifted her cup in a silent toast. "If you find the answers, I hope you'll share with the rest of us."

He smiled at her. "Maybe we can find them together."

Warmth bloomed in her chest and spread through her body in a lazy wave. "I'd like that," she said.

Julian's smile widened, then morphed into a frown as he caught sight of something over her shoulder.

"What is it?" Ruth turned to look out the window, but saw nothing unusual.

"Probably nothing," he muttered. "There was a car last night that drove by while Sam and I were talking. I thought I just saw it again now."

Ruth lifted one eyebrow. "There are a lot of cars in Copper Cove," she pointed out.

"True," Julian replied. "But not too many El Caminos."

"Do you think someone is following you?" It sounded ludicrous, like something out of a spy movie plot. But what if it was true? Was Julian in danger?

Please, Lord, keep him safe, she prayed silently.

He shook his head. "It's probably just a coincidence," he said. "Nothing to worry about."

"If you say so." She glanced at the manila file folder, still lying on the table between them. "What's in there?"

"This is part of the case file," Julian replied. "I brought it because I didn't know if you wanted to go through the material together."

Ruth nodded slowly. "That might actually be helpful. When Lily became my patient, I was granted access to her medical records. But aside from what she's told me and what the newspaper stories said, I don't know what happened that night."

Julian slid the file in front of her. "It's all in here."

She put her hand on the folder, but hesitated before opening it. "Are there… I mean, I don't really want to see…"

"I didn't include the crime scene photos," Julian said gently. "But the written reports are there."

"Thanks." She opened the folder and began to skim the documents, frowning as she read the descriptions.

Julian stepped away and returned with two apple fritters. He placed one plate near her and tucked into his own, sipping his coffee in silence, letting her process things at her own pace. It was nice just being near him, even if she was getting up to speed on the investigation into a double homicide.

And he was right—the pastry was delicious.

"So everyone assumed it was a home invasion gone bad?"

Julian nodded. "That was the consensus. Lily wasn't able to provide confirmation, but we know there was some jewelry taken, and based on the photos, we know an item from the bookshelves was removed."

"How could you possibly know that?"

Julian smiled. "Jim gets the credit for that. About six months prior to the murders, the local paper profiled the Pushkins' home in a spread. Kind of an architectural digest thing. Jim compared the crime scene photos to the ones that ran in the paper, and realized that an etched-glass globe was missing from the bookshelf."

"That's an odd thing to take," Ruth remarked.

"I always thought so, too," Julian said. "Especially

since there was some pretty expensive art on display, as well."

"Probably harder to sell that," Ruth said.

The corners of Julian's mouth twitched, and she got the impression he was amused. "Look at you, thinking like a criminal," he teased.

"I like to keep my options open," she replied. Then she remembered what they were talking about and grew serious again. "It looks like there were never any suspects identified?"

Julian's expression sobered. "That's right. There were a few leads, but they didn't pan out."

"Were there any other cases like this?" She didn't remember hearing anything about a spree of violent crimes, but perhaps she'd missed the news? After all, some days she had trouble remembering what she'd had for breakfast, much less things that had happened six years ago.

"There was a similar case in Phoenix a few months later, but they were able to make an arrest. It was clear the suspect in that case wasn't connected to the Pushkins."

"Jim must have been frustrated."

"I imagine he was," Julian said. "He always thought there was something else going on, but he was never able to prove it."

"And you agree with him?" It wasn't really a question: Ruth could tell by the way Julian talked about the case that he didn't think it was an accidental murder during a home invasion.

"Yeah," Julian confirmed. "I think Jim was onto

something. And now that Lily is remembering more of that night, we have a real shot at figuring it out."

"The gang," Ruth said, thinking out loud. "Even if Sam isn't involved, you said earlier they take jobs for people. Would something like this be considered a job?" She gestured to the file, repulsed by the idea of killing someone for money. But she wasn't totally naive. Maybe that was the connection Jim had been trying to make all along?

Julian nodded, a glint of respect in his eyes. "That's what I'm wondering myself."

"So if you figure out who might have hired them…"

"Then we've solved the mystery," he finished.

Ruth leaned forward. "Okay, so how do we do that?" The role of consultant was getting more and more interesting, and she was eager to help Julian in his investigation. It was almost like a jigsaw puzzle, but with some of the pieces missing. If only it weren't all so tragic.

Julian tilted his head to the side. "Well, it's not going to be easy," he said. "I know Lily's father was an attorney, so I'm going to check into the cases he was working on prior to his death. Jim did a little digging into that, but it's possible he missed something."

"What can I do?" Ruth asked. She wasn't a police officer, but maybe there was some way she could help Julian and, by extension, Lily?

"Keep working with Lily," Julian said. "If she remembers anything else, let me know as soon as possible."

She nodded. "I can do that. We have a session on Monday, in fact."

"Excellent." Julian took a sip of coffee and frowned.

"Cold?" Ruth guessed.

He nodded and took another sip. "Yeah. But caffeine is caffeine."

Ruth shook her head and started collecting the papers to put back into the folder. "I think you'd be better served by a nap this afternoon."

"No rest for the wicked," Julian said. "And this isn't my only case."

"Well, then, I won't keep you here any longer." Ruth gathered up her bag and empty cup and stood. Julian did the same, and together they walked to the door of the coffee shop.

"Thanks again, Ruth," he said as he held the door for her. "I'm glad we cleared things up. I feel a lot better now, knowing you don't hate me."

"I never hated you," she said, smiling up at him. "I was disappointed."

"That's worse," he joked.

"Maybe. But I'm not upset with you anymore. I'm sorry for my part in our misunderstanding. In the future, I promise to listen to you before storming off. Deal?"

He grinned, twin dimples appearing on his stubbled cheeks. "Deal." He stepped forward and folded her into a hug.

Ruth sucked in a breath as he pulled her toward him. His chest was hard and solid against her body, and she could feel the latent strength in his arms as they wrapped around her. The scent of his soap filled her nose—a crisp, clean note that made her think of sunshine. She briefly closed her eyes, wishing she could stay like this all day.

All too soon, Julian pulled back. His stubble rasped against her skin, and before she realized what was happening, he pressed his lips gently to the curve of her cheek.

Her heart jumped into her throat and her tongue felt tangled around itself. He smiled down at her, his brown eyes warm.

"Talk to you soon?" he asked.

She tried to say yes but a strangled squeak was all she could manage.

It must have sounded like an assent. Julian released her and they walked the few steps toward their vehicles. He'd parked next to her, so he waited for her to start her car before he drove away. She gave him a little wave, a flush creeping over her whole body as they went their separate ways.

"It was just a cheek kiss," she said to herself as she cranked up the air-conditioning. "Europeans do it all the time."

But not with Julian.

She smiled to herself as she headed home. Her mind was so filled with thoughts of the man that she never noticed the El Camino following her a few car lengths behind.

"Aguirre! Got a minute?"

Julian looked up at the summons and nodded. When the lieutenant called, you answered.

"What's up?" he asked as he strolled into his commander's office.

Lieutenant David Pierce gestured to the chair in front

of his desk. Julian took a seat and waited to hear the reason for this conversation.

"Any progress on the Pushkin case?"

The question wasn't unexpected. Even though it was only Monday, it wasn't unreasonable his boss wanted an update on the investigation. Julian had a reputation for working through weekends.

"Well, you've seen the sketch," Julian said. He briefly outlined his conversation with Sam, and the possible involvement of the Rising Suns gang.

Pierce frowned. "I don't need to tell you to step lightly there. I'll do a little digging on my end and see if I can find out what kind of case Sam is working. But if the Feds are involved, that's going to complicate things. You know how territorial people can be."

"I do," Julian replied. It was an issue he'd come up against a few times in his career so far. While he liked to think that the law enforcement community as a whole had the goal of stopping crime, the truth was that different agencies had different agendas. If his investigation put a federal case in jeopardy, he might be told to stand down so as not to endanger an active investigation. "Truth be told, if the gang is involved, I'm less interested in pinning the murders on them and more interested in finding out why they were there in the first place."

"You think this was a hired hit?"

"I wouldn't be surprised."

Pierce steepled his hands and rested his fingers on his chin. "Jim never thought it was a straight home invasion, either," he said, almost to himself. "We never could prove anything, but then again, the girl wasn't talking to us at that point."

She has a name, Julian thought. "Lily has been very helpful so far. And I think it's possible she'll continue to remember details from that night."

Pierce frowned. "It's gonna take more than her word," he said doubtfully.

Julian nodded. "I know. But she's already given me some new leads. This angle with the Rising Suns, for instance, came directly from her."

David leaned back in his chair and put his hands behind his head. "I always felt so bad for her. Jim was on-scene that night, and he told me about when the social worker took her away. She was this tiny little thing in pink princess pajamas, clutching her teddy bear."

Julian felt a heaviness descend on his heart as he imagined the moment. Lily was a strong, vibrant girl now, but at the time? She must have been terrified beyond measure.

"For what it's worth," he said quietly, "she's doing well now."

"I'm glad to hear that," Pierce said. "If anyone deserves a happy ending, it's her."

"Did Jim ever talk to you about the father?" Julian had read Jim's case notes dozens of times, but perhaps he'd talked things over with Pierce and mentioned something he hadn't written down?

The lieutenant frowned. "I'm sure he did, but I don't remember anything offhand. Why?"

Julian shrugged. "I'm looking at the father's work, trying to figure out if he was involved in any projects that may have angered the wrong people."

"He was a lawyer, right? Worked on contracts, if I recall."

"That's right." Julian leaned forward in his chair, hoping Pierce had something for him.

But the older man shook his head. "It's possible you're onto something. I can't imagine contract law is that interesting, but I suppose even mobsters and rich criminals have to play by the book sometimes."

"Maybe so," Julian replied. He didn't think this avenue was going to yield much, but he had to at least check it out. He'd already put calls in to the various charities Mrs. Pushkin had worked with, but so far, everything seemed aboveboard. Still, he knew that a squeaky-clean public reputation could hide a multitude of sins. Someone had wanted the Pushkins dead. That meant they likely had some skeletons in their closet.

Julian just had to find them.

"Anything else, Lieutenant?"

Pierce waved him away. "Just keep me posted. And let me know if you need my help with anything. I'll see what I can find out about Sam and get back to you."

"Thank you, sir," Julian said. "I appreciate it."

He walked out of the office and returned to his desk. The message light on his phone blinked red, indicating he'd missed a call. Maybe Ruth had called his office instead of his cell phone?

His mood perked up at the possibility. Even though he'd just seen her on Saturday, he wouldn't mind spending time with her again. It was funny, how quickly she'd become a regular in his thoughts. And now that he'd hugged her and kissed her, albeit only on the cheek, she was definitely a fixture in his mind.

Julian picked up the phone and dialed, disappoint-
ment washing over him as he listened to the message.
The public defender's office had a question about a case
Julian had worked several months ago. It wasn't a time-
sensitive issue, so he'd call them back later.

He put the phone down but his hand lingered on
the receiver, near the keypad. Should he call Ruth? He
knew she was meeting with Lily today. Had the girl remembered anything else? A sense of urgency nipped at
him, prodding him to make the call. But he took a deep
breath and focused on his computer instead. Bugging
Ruth for an update might make him feel like he was
doing something, but it would only cause her stress.
Besides, he wasn't sure what time she and Lily were
meeting. They may not have even talked yet.

"Cool it, Aguirre," he muttered.

It was difficult for Julian to relax at the moment. Not
only was it a high-profile cold case, but he felt like he
owed it to Jim to find the killer once and for all. His
anxiety made him feel like every minute he wasn't ac-
tively doing *something* was time wasted, time that might
make the difference in solving this mystery. Logically,
he knew that wasn't the case; investigations moved at
their own pace, and he needed to let things unfold. If he
pushed too hard, tried too much, the chances he would
make a mistake increased.

Bringing Ruth on as a consultant had been a good
idea. He'd initially done it to salvage their personal connection, but after their meeting on Saturday, Julian realized how much he enjoyed talking things over with a
partner. And while Ruth wasn't a cop, she still made a
good sounding board for his ideas.

Even more surprising? He trusted her. That wasn't just his attraction to her talking, either. Julian had taken a gamble showing her some of the case files. But based on her reactions, he knew he hadn't made a mistake. Ruth was even more invested in helping him now, which made her a great ally.

So if Lily did give her new information today, he was confident Ruth would tell him about it as soon as she could.

The realization helped calm some of his nerves, but his stomach still churned.

Julian opened his desk drawer, looking for a roll of antacids. While he searched, he found the iPod he'd stashed here after a workout in the building's gym. He found the medicine, and on a whim, he pulled out the iPod. He considered the device while he crunched on the chalky tablets. What could it hurt?

Another search turned up some headphones, and in no time at all, Julian had queued up some orchestral music. Mozart. His dad used to put it on during Sunday afternoons while he napped on the recliner. Julian braced himself, uncertain how he would feel hearing the familiar music after all this time.

He needn't have worried. The music wrapped around him like an old blanket, comforting and warm. As the sounds of the instruments filled his ears, he felt some of the tension leave his body. Memories of his father drifted to the surface, images from a simpler, happier time when the world hadn't seemed so complicated. Before his father's sins had come to light.

After a moment, Julian turned back to his computer,

the music helping to quiet the voice in his mind so he could focus.

While he worked, Ruth's face appeared in his mind's eye and Julian felt a rush of warmth. He didn't know how it worked, and he didn't know why it was affecting him so powerfully, but he couldn't deny listening to music had changed his whole mood. It was as though the sounds had reset his system, taking away some of his stress so he could get through the rest of his day.

I get it now.

And he couldn't wait to share his realization with Ruth.

Chapter Six

"Miss Ruth? I think I want to try to write a song."

Ruth smiled at Lily, pleased to hear her interest in music was growing. "I think that's a wonderful idea."

Lily frowned. "The thing is, I don't really know how to do it."

"Ah." Ruth took a seat on the sofa and patted the cushion next to her. Lily walked over and sat, holding the tambourine she'd picked up after walking into Ruth's office.

"The thing about songwriting is that there are many ways to do it. There's no formula—you just have to figure out what works for you."

"What do you mean?" Lily tilted her head to the side.

"Well…" Ruth searched her brain for examples. "Take the Rolling Stones, for instance. They usually wrote the music first, then came up with words to fit the beat."

Lily wrinkled her nose. "Who?"

Ruth tried not to wince, suddenly feeling a thousand years old. "Never mind." She shook her head, pushing aside the reflexive dismay that accompanied this un-expected reminder of her age. She tried again. "You know Taylor Swift?"

Lily nodded, her face brightening. "Oh, yeah. Of course."

"I read that she keeps a journal," Ruth said. "She writes down ideas and phrases and uses them when she's writing her songs."

"So the music part comes later?" Lily sounded almost hopeful.

"I think sometimes it does," Ruth confirmed.

Lily leaned back against the sofa, seeming to relax. "That's good. I don't really know how to write music, but I've been keeping a journal."

"That's great!" Ruth had suggested journaling as a way for Lily to process her feelings. It was nice to know the girl had taken the suggestion to heart. "Has writing helped you?"

"I guess so." Lily shrugged. "I mean, I like writing. It's kind of nice, because I can put down whatever I want."

"It's totally up to you," Ruth said.

Lily nodded. "I usually put on some music." She glanced at Ruth. "I made a playlist of some of the songs we've listened to together, and sometimes when I'm feeling stressed, it helps me relax."

Warmth spread through Ruth's chest. "I'm very glad to hear that."

"It's funny," Lily continued. "But sometimes when I hear those songs, it makes me feel like I'm here in your office with you. Like I can even smell the candles you sometimes light. And if I close my eyes, I feel like I'm sitting on the couch. Like I am now." She laughed. "Am I making sense?"

Ruth nodded. "Yes," she said firmly. "That's what makes music so special. It can take you to another place with just a few notes."

"Yeah." Lily was silent a moment, thinking. "Where does it take you?" she finally asked.

Ruth shrugged. "That depends on the song, really. Sometimes, I'll hear a song that reminds me of a night out with friends. Other times, I'll play Barbra Streisand and be transported back to when I was a kid and my mom would play her music while she cleaned the house on the weekends." The remembered scent of lemon polish filled her nose as she inhaled, just the mention of the music enough to stir up the memories.

Lily looked thoughtful. "I think my grandma has some of her CDs," she said doubtfully.

"Probably," Ruth said dryly. "What about you, though? You said some songs make you feel like you're here. What else do you like to listen to?"

"Well…" Lily trailed off, and a faint pink blush spread across her cheeks. "Sometimes I'll play Christmas carols."

"Okay," Ruth said encouragingly. Lots of people liked Christmas carols. So why did Lily seem embarrassed by the admission? "What about those songs is special to you?"

"My mom used to sing them to me," Lily said simply.

Understanding rolled over Ruth and she fought the impulse to gather Lily in a hug. "I see," she said, nodding. "So when you miss your mom you listen to Christmas carols?"

Lily nodded. "I know it's silly—"

"No," Ruth interrupted. "It's not. Don't ever let anyone tell you differently."

Lily nodded, and Ruth hoped she was taking her words to heart.

"So, is there like a class I can take to learn how to write a song?" she asked, changing the subject.

Ruth rolled with it. "There are classes. I can ask around and find out if there are any good ones in the area. There's always the internet, too."

Lily frowned. "I don't think my grandparents would like that. They're pretty strict about my computer time."

"I understand," Ruth said. "If you like, I can talk to them about it. They might change their minds if they know it's for a class."

"Maybe," Lily replied. But her tone was heavy with doubt. "Do you want to see some of what I've written? Maybe you can tell me if it's any good?"

"Of course!" Ruth leaned forward, anticipation thrumming through her as Lily opened the bag at her feet and withdrew a pink journal. She passed it to Ruth readily enough, but as Ruth took it, Lily held on.

"It's okay if you don't think my songs are any good," she said and held Ruth's gaze. "I'd rather hear it from you than from someone else."

Ruth's heart cracked as she looked at Lily. "Sweetheart, I'm sure your songs are great. And it doesn't matter what I think, or what anyone else thinks, either. Music is subjective. The important thing is that *you* like your songs. That they mean something to you. Even if you never share them with anyone else, the fact that you wrote them makes them special."

Lily gave her a small smile. "Thanks."

"Thank you for trusting me enough to share."

Lily released her hold on the book, and Ruth took it into her lap. "Where should I start?" She was honored that Lily was sharing, but she didn't want to invade the girl's privacy. Just because she'd agreed to show her songs didn't mean she wanted the rest of her journal to be read.

Lily slid across the sofa until she was sitting right next to Ruth. She reached over and opened the journal, flipping through a few pages until she landed on one written in bright purple ink.

"The purple makes me happy," she explained.

Ruth smiled. "Naturally."

Lily seemed to hold her breath while Ruth read through the lyrics. It was a simple enough song, about a boy in her class. But Ruth could tell Lily had poured her emotions into it. There were several parts that had been scratched out, with new words written in the margins. Lily had doodled some hearts and stars along the edges of the paper, likely while brainstorming. Overall, it was a touching example of a young girl coming to terms with a crush.

Ruth turned to Lily. "I think this is wonderful," she said honestly. "You've done a nice job here, with the rhyming and the rhythm of the lyrics. Was this your first song?"

Lily shook her head. "No. I've been practicing a bit. That one is a fun song. I have others that aren't so nice."

Something about the girl's tone made the hairs prick up on the back of Ruth's neck. "May I see them?"

Lily shrugged. "Sure. It's nothing we haven't already

talked about before." She flipped through more of the pages, this time stopping at one written in red and black.

As soon as Ruth began reading, she understood the choice of ink color. This song was dark and emotional, full of torment and anguish. With just a few words, Lily conveyed a helpless terror that seemed to vibrate off the page.

Ruth swallowed and glanced at Lily. The girl was watching her carefully, studying her reaction. "This reads like one of your nightmares," Ruth said softly.

Lily nodded. "I wrote it after I woke up from one," she confirmed. "I can't show it to my grandparents."

"Do you still feel this way?" Ruth ran her finger over an especially graphic passage, hoping the act of writing had eased Lily's anxiety.

"Sometimes?" Lily shook her head. "I don't know. It's hard to say. Some days are great, and other times I feel like I'm back under the bed again, watching it happen."

"What do you do when you feel like that?" Ruth had been trying to teach Lily techniques to help her cope with the bad days, things she could try to lift herself out of the darkness. Were they working? Or did she need to come up with a different strategy?

"I write." Lily gestured to the journal. "Or I put on music. Or call a friend."

Ruth let out a breath she didn't realize she'd been holding. "That's good. Those are all positive ways of dealing with your thoughts and emotions."

"I even draw sometimes." Lily reached over and started flipping through the journal once more, turning the pages to reveal a series of sketches. It was clear she wasn't an artist, but she'd tried to draw faces and animals.

Ruth examined the drawings, guessing Lily's emotional state based on the colors she'd used. This page had bright, cheerful colors. But as she turned to the next, it was full of black, red and shades of gray.

"Bad day?" she asked, pointing to it.

Lily shrugged. "Yeah."

Ruth went to turn the page, but something in the corner caught her eye. She squinted, bringing the journal closer to her face so she could see.

In the bottom left corner, tucked almost into the spine of the book, was a name written in red ink with a question mark.

Eric?

Ruth pointed to the word. "Lily, who's Eric?"

Lily's face went pale. "Um, I don't know." She reached for the journal and Ruth surrendered it immediately. Lily snapped it shut and shoved it back into her bag.

Ruth waited until Lily looked at her again. "You're not in trouble," she said softly. "And you know I'm not going to try to force you to talk to me."

Lily looked down but didn't speak.

"I hope you know you can trust me," she continued. "If Eric is someone who hurt you, you don't have to protect him." Ruth's mind raced as she considered possibilities. Was he a teacher or coach at school? A kid from her class? Had someone abused Lily, or tried to? Her heart clenched at the thought. Hadn't the girl already been through enough in her young life?

"I'm not protecting anyone," Lily said. Her voice sounded very small, and it was clear she was upset.

"Okay," Ruth said easily. "I'm glad to hear that. Is Eric someone you know from school?"

"No." Lily shook her head. For a moment, it looked like she wasn't going to speak again. Then she glanced at Ruth. "I don't know who he is."

"What made you decide to write his name in your journal?" Based on the placement on the page, and the fact she'd written in red and black ink, Ruth knew that whoever Eric was, he'd upset Lily. Possibly even scared her. But why?

"I needed to get it out of my head," Lily said finally. "I keep hearing this name in my dreams. I feel like I should know who this is, but I don't."

"Who is saying the name?" Ruth asked. If they could identify who was speaking, perhaps Lily would feel better.

Lily shook her head. "That's just it. I don't know."

"Is it a woman or a man who says the name?" Ruth probed gently.

"A man," Lily said right away. "He's got a mean voice."

"What else is happening in your dreams when you hear this name?"

Lily frowned. "I can't see anything." She got a far-away look in her eyes, clearly remembering. "It's like something is over my face, and I feel hot, like something is on top of me. Like I'm covered in blankets."

"Like you're under a bed?" Ruth suggested softly.

Lily blinked at her, surprise dawning on her face. "Yeah, actually. How'd you know?"

"Just a guess," Ruth replied. "So you hear a mean voice say this name. Then what happens?"

Lily shrugged. "Then I hear a laugh. But not a nice laugh. A cruel laugh. Does that make sense?"

Ruth nodded. "Yes."

"And then I wake up." She looked at Ruth, her expression defeated. "That's it. I don't know what it means, I don't know who he is. I don't know anything!" Her voice rose as she spoke, full of frustration and despair.

"It's okay," Ruth said soothingly. "You don't have to have all the answers. I just don't want you to feel like you need to carry this around inside you."

"That's why I wrote it down," Lily said dully. "I thought it would help get his name out of my head. But I still hear it sometimes."

Ruth felt a tingling along her spine as a new possibility occurred to her. "Do you think you're remembering something? That you actually heard a man say this name before?"

"Maybe." Lily pushed a strand of hair behind her ear. "But I don't hear it when I have my usual nightmares about that night. This is a separate dream."

"I understand," Ruth replied. "I don't think dreams have to be all or nothing. There's no rule that says your memories can't come in different dreams."

"So you think this is part of what happened that night? That I heard someone say 'Eric' and laugh?"

"I don't know," Ruth replied honestly. "But I think we should probably tell Jul—" She caught herself at the last second. "I think we should tell Detective Aguirre about this, don't you?"

Lily nodded. "Yeah, you're probably right. I just don't want him to get mad at me."

Ruth blinked, caught off guard by the girl's response. "Why would you think he'd be angry?" She searched her memories, trying to come up with any moment where Julian might have given Lily the impression he'd be upset with her. Nothing came immediately to mind, but was it possible she'd missed something? Had her attraction to Julian meant she'd overlooked a sign?

Lily's eyes shone as she looked up at Ruth. "For not telling him before. I just didn't think it was important."

And there it was. Nothing Julian had said or done, just Lily's overwhelming sense of responsibility making her feel like she wasn't doing enough to solve her parents' murder. Once again, Ruth felt her heart ache for Lily and the struggles she faced. In some ways, she could relate to the girl. After her sister's death, Ruth had felt responsible. What if they hadn't been crossing the street? What if she'd walked just a little bit faster? What if…what if?

Ruth reached out and pulled Lily in for a hug. "No one is going to be mad at you, least of all the detective." She gave Lily a squeeze, then released her. "He appreciates your help, and he doesn't expect you to know everything."

Lily sniffed. "Okay."

Ruth wanted to give the girl another hug, but held herself back. As much as she cared for Lily, she had to remember she was her therapist, not her friend.

Still, she wanted to help Lily. "Did I ever tell you about my sister?"

Lily shook her head. "No. I didn't know you have a sister."

"Her name was Mary," Ruth began. She told Lily about the car accident, and how Mary had pushed her out of the way but been hit herself. Ruth left out the part about the off-duty police officer, and the way he'd escaped justice.

"That's so sad," Lily said after Ruth had finished the story.

Ruth nodded. "I miss her every day. But you know, in the beginning, I blamed myself for what had happened."

Lily didn't respond, but Ruth could tell by her expression that she was listening intently.

"I had nightmares," Ruth continued. "I thought if I had acted differently, or if we had been walking another way, the accident wouldn't have happened and Mary would still be alive."

"Did your parents blame you?" Lily's voice was quiet, barely above a whisper.

"No." Ruth shook her head. "They knew I wasn't responsible. See, I felt like I could have done more, but I was a kid myself. There was no way I should have known what to do or how to respond, and my parents knew that."

"I'm glad," Lily said. "It wasn't your fault."

"I know that now," Ruth replied. "And the thing is, Lily, what happened to your parents isn't your fault, either."

Lily looked away. "I know that," she said flatly.

"Do you?" Ruth asked. "The way you're talking now makes me wonder if some part of you feels like you should have done something."

Lily's breath shuddered. "I just watched it happen. I didn't try to stop them."

"Of course not!" Ruth leaned forward and took one of Lily's hands. "You were four years old, Lily. They were grown men. There was nothing you could do to protect your parents. In fact, if you had tried, those men would have killed you, too!"

"My mom saw me." Lily spoke as though Ruth hadn't said anything. "I never told anyone this, but she saw me. After they..." She trailed off, grimaced. "After she fell to the floor, her face was turned so she could look down the hall. I think she saw me hiding under the bed, because she smiled and whispered something."

Ruth could imagine the scene easily, the details fresh in her mind after her recent perusal of the case files. "I'm sure she was relieved to know you were safe."

"But what if she was asking me to help her?" Lily met Ruth's eyes, anguish etched on her young face. "What if she wanted me to do something, and I didn't?"

Ruth took a deep breath, knowing she had to be careful. It was clear Lily was haunted by this memory, and Ruth wanted to bring her peace. But if she came on too strong, dismissed Lily's fears out of hand, Lily wouldn't believe anything she said.

Please help me, Ruth prayed silently. She needed guidance right now, needed to be shown the right path forward. This moment was too important to mess up.

"I'm not a mother," Ruth started. "But I know many women who are. And every single one of them would sacrifice themselves to protect their child, no matter how old their child was."

Lily remained silent.

"I don't think your mom was asking you for help," Ruth continued. "I think she was saying something very different."

"Like what?" Lily gave her a cautious look, her body tense as she braced to hear what Ruth was going to say.

The answer hit Ruth like a flash of light, dissolving her doubts in an instant. "I think she was saying, 'I love you.'"

Lily digested that for a moment, her brows drawn together as she considered the possibility. "You really think so?"

Ruth nodded, certainty filling her. "Oh, yes. I know if I saw my child as I was dying, my last act would be to tell them how much I love them. I'm positive your mom was doing the same."

"Maybe you're right." Ruth could tell by Lily's tone she didn't quite believe her, but at least she seemed to be thinking about it. While Ruth wished Lily would stop blaming herself for what had happened, at least she had planted this seed today. She'd make sure to tend to it during later sessions, and hopefully one day Lily would realize she wasn't at all responsible for the events of that horrible night.

"You can tell the detective about that memory, too," Lily said shyly. "If you think it will help."

Ruth shook her head. "That one is special. I don't think he needs to know about it."

A look of relief flashed across Lily's face. "Do you need to take my journal to show him?" She sounded reluctant to part with it, and Ruth could understand why. It was a highly personal thing, and the idea of strangers reading her words had to make Lily feel a bit anxious.

"I don't think he'll need to see the whole thing," Ruth said. "But can I take a picture of the page with the name?"

Lily nodded and pulled the book from her bag once more. "Sure." She passed it back to Ruth. "I mean, if he needs to read it, it's okay I guess. I just…" She trailed off and Ruth smiled.

"I get it," she said. "It's hard to share your thoughts with people sometimes. I think a picture will be enough for now."

"Okay." Lily flipped back to the page in question, and Ruth used her phone to snap an image. She made sure to take a picture of the drawings on the page, as well. She couldn't really decipher what they were, but maybe Julian might think they were of use to the investigation?

The session wrapped up quickly after that, and Ruth gave Lily a parting hug at the door. Then she slipped her phone into her pocket and headed for the bathroom.

She stared at her reflection in the mirror as she washed her hands, but she didn't really see her own face. Instead, Lily's voice echoed in her mind, her imagination bringing the girl's words about her mother's dying moments to life.

Ruth shuddered and took a deep breath, trying to cast out the disturbing thoughts. Normally, she didn't have a problem maintaining a professional distance from her patients, but Lily was different. She cared deeply about the girl, and hearing about the last memory she had of her mother had nearly broken Ruth's heart.

She sighed and leaned against the sink. Ruth had learned early on that she couldn't schedule any appointments after meeting with Lily—she was just too emotionally wrung out to be of any help to her other patients after these sessions. Thankfully, that meant she could leave for the day.

But before she went home, she'd stop at the police station. She needed to tell Julian what Lily had shown her today, and share her dream about hearing the voice. The knowledge that she would soon see Julian again helped lift her spirits, and she headed back to her office feeling a bit better.

She walked to her desk to shut down her computer and froze. A chill raced through her veins as she stared down at the note that was lying across her keyboard.

Shut the brat up, or we'll finish what we started.

Julian half jogged, half walked down the hospital corridor that led to Ruth's office. He wanted to break out into a run but decided that wouldn't go over well; the other people in the hall were already giving him worried looks as he sped past.

Gone was the earlier sense of peace that had been brought about by listening to music. As soon as he'd picked up the phone and heard Ruth's voice, he'd known something was wrong.

She'd insisted she was fine, that there was nothing to worry about. But after hearing the contents of the anonymous note left on her desk, Julian hadn't hesitated to jump in his truck and head to the hospital. Ruth might not think she was in danger, but he knew better.

He rounded the corner now and caught sight of her office door ahead on the right. Out of habit, he glanced up, checking the ceiling of the corridor for security cameras. He spied one, farther down the hall, closer to the next corner. He bit his lip, making a mental note to check the recording. The camera might be too far away from Ruth's office to identify whoever had left the note on her desk, but it was worth a shot.

Julian stopped and knocked loudly on her office door. He'd told her to close and lock it until he arrived, and seeing she had followed his instructions made him relax a bit.

"Ruth? It's Julian."

He heard the muffled sound of footsteps approach. The handle wiggled a bit as she fumbled with the lock, and then she had the door open.

Relief washed over her face when she saw him, making him feel ten feet tall and bulletproof. Under any other circumstances, Julian would have enjoyed the boost to his ego—there was something deeply satisfying about the woman he was attracted to calling him when she needed help. But this wasn't a regular, run-of-the-mill problem. Ruth and Lily were both in danger, and it was his job to keep them safe.

She gestured for him to come inside, then shut the door behind him and flipped the lock, sealing them in together.

"Are you okay?" he asked.

Ruth nodded, but she wouldn't meet his eyes. She started to walk over to her desk, her gait stiff and a little halting.

She's scared, he realized. She had talked a good game on the phone, but sometime between their call and his arrival, Ruth had gotten spooked. It was clear the shock of discovering the note had worn off, and now she was rattled by its implications. Julian mentally kicked himself for not getting here sooner. If he'd driven a little bit faster, decided to run instead of jog, he might have been here for her.

He'd just have to settle for helping her now.

"Ruth."

She stopped and he took a step toward her. "Come here," he said softly.

She remained still, but didn't protest when he moved in close and circled his arms around her.

For a second, she stood stiffly in his embrace. Then a shudder went through her body and she melted against his chest. Her arms snaked around him, clutching his shoulders tightly as she pressed her forehead to his shoulder.

"It's okay," he said quietly, running one hand up and down her back in light strokes. Anger built in his chest as he comforted her. Ruth was a good person; she didn't deserve to be targeted like this, to be threatened for trying to help an innocent girl.

"Someone has been watching us," she said, her voice tight with emotion. "They've been watching me and Lily, and they know she's talking to you. They know she's told you things."

"I won't let them hurt you or her," Julian said.

"How can you say that?" Ruth pulled back, her eyes bright with fear. "I don't even know who left this note! But they were here." She trembled a bit, her fingers digging into the fabric of his shirt. "They were here, Julian. Spying on me. On Lily and me. They could have come in during our session and…" Her voice faded as she shook her head. "They were here, and I didn't even know it!"

"I understand," Julian said. Every protective instinct in his body insisted he sweep Ruth into his arms and carry her off to an undisclosed location, one where he could keep watch over her and make sure no one got close enough to harm her. But that wasn't a practical solution. No matter how much he might want to hide her away from the world, the fact was she had to live her life.

"You have to protect Lily." Ruth slid her hands to his forearms, gripping him with an intensity that matched her words. "Can you send her to witness protection or something?"

"Not exactly," Julian said. Ruth glared at him, clearly unhappy with his response. "Why don't you show me the note?" he suggested, changing the subject slightly. "I've already dispatched a car to park in front of Lily's house, and they'll wait there until I figure out what to do."

Ruth nodded, some of the fight going out of her now that she knew Lily was safe for the moment. "I left it on my desk," she said, gesturing. "I didn't even touch it. I was hoping you could get fingerprints off it or something?"

"That's good," Julian said absently as he read the note. It was short and to the point. The handwriting was on the messy side of legible, which only enhanced the sinister quality of the message. *Like a ransom note in a movie.*

He glanced around the desk, then widened his gaze

to Ruth's office. "Was anything disturbed when you returned from the bathroom?"

She shook her head. "Not that I noticed. I looked around after we spoke, and I still don't see anything out of place. Just the note."

"How long were you gone?"

She shrugged. "Maybe five minutes?"

"And you didn't notice anyone leaving your office, or see anyone in the hallway as you walked back?"

"No."

Julian nodded, the wheels turning in his head as he considered everything she'd told him. Ruth stood next to him, chewing on her thumbnail as she stared down at the desk.

"Let's sit down," he suggested. Staring at that note would only make her more anxious.

He led her to the sofa and they both sat. "Here's what I'm thinking," he said. "Whoever did this is trying to scare you. If they'd wanted to hurt you, they would have hidden in your office and waited for you to return. If they'd wanted to hurt Lily, they would have acted while you were in session or soon after, maybe when she was in the parking lot with her grandparents. This is a warning shot, designed to make you think twice before meeting with her again."

"Well, it's working," Ruth muttered. "I don't want to be the reason she gets hurt."

"Of course not," Julian said. "But are you really going to terminate her therapy because of this threat?"

Ruth gaped at him. "What other choice do I have?" She pointed to her desk. "They said they would 'finish the job.' I can only assume they're talking about her parents, and that they'll come back and kill her if she keeps talking to me."

"I'm sure that's exactly what they want you to think," Julian said. A tingle of excitement shot down his spine as his thoughts began to coalesce. "But you can't give in to their demands."

Ruth shook her head as though she hadn't heard him. "What? Are you serious?"

"Yes." He leaned forward, adrenaline building in his system. "Don't you see? We must be onto something. If we assume the people who killed Lily's parents left this note, it's clear they're spooked. I've only spoken to her twice, but they must think she's given me valuable information. They're hoping to scare her off, keep her from saying more."

Awareness dawned on Ruth's face. "If that's the case, it means her parents didn't die in a random home invasion gone wrong. It means your partner was right all along—the Pushkins were deliberately targeted that night."

Julian nodded, a sense of certainty growing in his chest. "Exactly. And whoever is responsible for their deaths has been keeping an eye on Lily. She wasn't a threat when she was younger. But now that she's starting to talk…"

Ruth was quiet for a moment. "I hate to say it, but I don't understand why they don't just kill her. Why bother to send these anonymous threats? If Lily's dead, there's no danger of her exposing them."

"They didn't have to worry last time," Julian said bluntly. "We didn't have enough leads and the investigation fizzled out. That doesn't usually happen. And whoever is behind this has to know that if Lily Push-kin is murdered, it will be a high-profile case. All of our resources will be brought to bear on the ensuing investigation. There's no way to guarantee they'd get away with murder a second time."

"So better to hide in the shadows than strike again and be caught?" Ruth said.

Julian nodded. "Exactly."

"What if this is the only warning?" Ruth glanced to her desk again and bit her bottom lip, clearly still worried. "What if Lily and I continue to meet, and the next time they decide to act? I'll never forgive myself if something happens to her."

"It's a possibility." Julian wasn't going to lie. He respected Ruth too much to use empty words to try to make her feel better. "I can't guarantee that won't happen. Especially since we don't know who delivered this note. But I'm hoping you'll still work with Lily."

Ruth eyed him warily. "Why's that?"

Julian took a deep breath, knowing Ruth probably wasn't going to like what he had to say. "I'm hoping to use your sessions with her to draw out the killers. If they see you're still talking to her, they'll have to assume she's talking about the murders. They won't be able to sit back and let that happen. They'll be forced to act."

For a moment, Ruth didn't respond. When she did speak, her voice was flat. "You want to use her as bait."

He knew it sounded bad. But what other choice did they have? He decided to change tactics a bit.

"Does Lily still need you?"

Ruth blinked, taken aback by the question. "I think so," she said cautiously.

"So she's still benefiting from your sessions together," Julian said.

Ruth nodded, appearing more confident now that he'd clarified his question. "Yes, I think she is. She's showing great improvement in her ability to handle her nightmares, and she's deploying several of the techniques we've explored to cope with harmful memories and the emotions they stir up."

Listening to Ruth talk, Julian could hear the passion she had for her job and her patients. Especially Lily. It was clear Ruth cared deeply for the girl and wanted the best for her. Admiration swelled in his chest as she continued to talk about her sessions with Lily; although Ruth and Lily seemed to have a special bond, he didn't doubt that Ruth put the same energy into helping all her patients. It was a testament to her character and work ethic, and he enjoyed hearing about her approach.

He waited for her to finish, then asked, "So if you'd never received this note, you would still want to meet with her?"

"Yes," Ruth said. "But," she continued, before he could speak, "I can't ignore this message."

"I'm not asking you to," Julian said. "I'm not suggesting we pretend like this never happened. I want you to continue your sessions, and I'll make sure there are plainclothes officers nearby. If there's any whiff of something amiss, they'll be in position to intervene."

Ruth tilted her head to the side. "What about when she's at home? The people who killed her parents aren't stupid—they've gotten away with it for this long. Do you really think they'd try to hurt her in such a public place?"

He'd anticipated this question. "I'll keep officers stationed outside her house, too." *And yours also*, he added silently. He didn't want to scare Ruth, but if the killers thought Lily was telling Ruth information about the murders, it was logical they'd want to silence her, as well.

"For how long?" Ruth shot back. "What happens if the leads dry up again? I can't imagine your boss will be pleased with your plan to park a couple of officers outside of one home indefinitely."

"You let me worry about that," Julian said. It was definitely something he'd have to address, but at this point, Julian had to believe he'd catch another break in the case before too long. The thought of the trail going cold again was too depressing to contemplate…

He could tell by the way Ruth was looking at him that she was considering his plan. He resisted the urge to keep talking—better to let her arrive at her decision in her own time, without any pressure from him. So he kept his mouth shut, mentally crossing his fingers that she would agree with his proposed course of action. If not…well, he'd have to come up with another idea.

"All right," she said finally. "I agree that Lily needs to continue therapy, and I don't like the idea of abruptly cutting her off without explanation. But using her as bait to draw the bad guys out into the open—I'm not comfortable doing that unless she knows and agrees to participate."

Julian breathed a sigh of relief. "I think you're right. She deserves to know what's happening."

"And if she says she wants no part of it? If she wants to stop meeting with me?" Ruth lifted one eyebrow in challenge, and Julian got the feeling she was testing him.

"Then you stop," he said simply. "I'm not going to force her to take part in this. God knows she's been through enough already."

"Yes," Ruth murmured. "He certainly does."

"Do you trust me to talk to her about it myself?" he asked.

"I do," Ruth replied. "But let's go together. If Lily does want to participate in your plan, I think her grandparents will be worried. You might make more progress talking to them if I'm there."

"I think you're right." It was the truth, but more importantly, it gave Julian an excuse to stay with Ruth for a little longer. He didn't like the idea of her being on her own, especially now that he knew someone involved with the Pushkin murders was watching her closely. She might not be the primary target right now, but that could change quickly. Julian didn't want to leave her unprotected if her name was moved up someone's hit list.

"I need a few minutes to take some pictures and bag the note." He didn't know if they'd get any fingerprints off the paper, but it was worth a shot. Maybe the lab would be able to find a match and provide him with a name. Unlikely, but you never knew, right?

Julian glanced at Ruth as he set to work. She'd regained her composure, but he could tell by the way her eyebrows were drawn together that she was worried. He didn't have the heart to tell her she should be.

God, You don't have to help me, he prayed as he worked. *But what about her? Will I be able to keep her safe?*

Julian wasn't expecting an answer. But at that moment, Ruth caught his eye. "It's going to be okay," she said matter-of-factly.

His skin tingled. If he didn't know better, he would've thought she'd read his mind. "I thought that was my line," he joked.

She smiled. "Maybe so. But it's true."

A sense of calm washed over him as he held her gaze. Was this his answer? Had his prayer actually been heard?

Julian didn't know what to think, but he had to admit he was intrigued. Still, there would be time for such examinations later. Right now, he had a job to do.

"I hope you're right," he said softly.

Chapter Seven

"Absolutely not!"

George Pushkin shoved his chair back from the dining room table and rose to his feet, his face flushed with emotion. Gone was the normally mild-mannered man who had answered the door only moments ago, ushering them inside with a polite greeting and an offer of a beverage.

Ruth glanced at Julian, wondering how he was going to handle this reaction. They'd ridden to the Pushkin home together, and on the way they'd discussed this very scenario. Ruth had thought it likely Lily's grandparents wouldn't want to put the girl at any greater risk, and Julian had agreed with her. Neither one of them wanted to see her get hurt, but at the same time, Ruth understood Julian's perspective. This case had been stalled for so long, and he was hungry for a chance to solve the mystery. She didn't blame him for wanting to move forward.

But she herself was torn. Part of her wanted to get things over with—to draw the killers out and see them arrested and brought to justice. Lily and her grandparents would finally get some closure and be able to move on with their lives.

But what if this plan backfired? What if they were successful in luring the murderers into the open and Julian didn't intervene in time to save Lily? Would Ruth be able to live with herself if her actions played a part in this girl coming to harm?

She'd prayed silently on the way over, hoping for guidance. Now she just had to be open to the response, whatever it turned out to be.

Julian opened his mouth to reply to the older man, but it was Lily's grandmother who intervened. "Sit down, George," she instructed. "They're not the ones you're mad at."

Ruth shot her a grateful smile and the woman nodded slightly. George pressed his lips together in a thin line, but he took his seat once more.

"You were saying?" Margaret nodded to Julian, encouraging him to continue.

Julian looked from her to her husband, clearly trying to gauge the mood. "Ah, yes, ma'am," he replied. "Well, the thing is, I'd like for Lily to continue her sessions with Ruth." He angled his head toward her in acknowledgment. "Ruth told me Lily benefits from their time together, and I don't want her to miss out on that."

"Neither do we," George said. His clipped delivery made it clear he was still struggling to contain himself. "But not if it puts her in danger."

"That's just it," Julian said. He leaned forward a bit, placing his hands on the table. "I'll have officers stationed all around the hospital and some close to Ruth's office. They'll be in civilian clothes, so they won't stick out. If anyone tries to approach the office while she's there, they'll be apprehended."

"But what about here?" Margaret asked. Ruth glanced at her, taking in the strain lines at the corners of her eyes and lips. Margaret Pushkin wasn't going to have an outburst like her husband, but she was plainly just as worried.

"Julian will station officers outside your home to keep you all safe," Ruth said. She had been reassured by his plan, but would Lily's family feel the same way?

George scoffed. "You mean like those kids in the car outside?" He pointed in the direction of the window, indicating the squad car parked at the curb. "I hardly think two young men who are barely old enough to shave are going to intimidate a murderer."

Ruth felt Julian stiffen next to her. She placed a hand on his forearm and gave him a gentle squeeze.

"Mr. Pushkin," Julian said, very calmly. "I appreciate that some of our officers look young, but I assure you, the men outside are fully qualified and trained to protect your family."

"Of course they are," Margaret said, glaring at her husband.

George scowled back, but after a few seconds of this silent standoff, he sighed. "When you get to be my age, Detective, everyone looks like a kid."

Julian's muscles relaxed under Ruth's hand. "I understand, sir. But please know I meant what I said—we will do everything possible to keep you safe."

Margaret shifted in her chair, and Ruth turned to her. "What are you thinking, Mrs. Pushkin?"

"Margaret," the older woman replied automatically. She pushed her glasses up her nose and regarded Ruth and Julian. "I just don't know," she said, shaking her head. "It's not that I don't trust you." She sounded apologetic as she looked at Julian. "But we've already lost our son, and Lily's mother was like a daughter to us. I'm not sure we can risk losing Lily, too."

"This is a hard decision," Ruth said quietly. Her heart went out to the couple; their desire to bring their son's killer to justice was being pitted against their need to keep their granddaughter safe. There was no easy choice to be made here.

"Do you think whoever left the note will really leave Lily alone if she stops going to therapy and stops talking to you?" The color had left George's face; he was much calmer now as he spoke.

"No," Julian said shortly. "I'm sorry, I know that's not what you wanted to hear. But if this note is real, and not just some kind of sick prank, the people who killed your son and his wife aren't going to suddenly start playing nice."

"Then why leave the note at all?" George asked, frowning.

Ruth answered him. "That was my question, too," she said. "We think they're trying to scare you all because they can't be sure they'd get away with murder a second time."

"And if I'm right," Julian continued, "I think your son was targeted. Someone wanted him killed. The people who pulled the trigger were just hired mercenaries. They aren't going to stick their necks out again unless they get paid for it."

"So the person who's really behind this hasn't ordered them to act?" Margaret asked.

Julian nodded. "I believe that's the case, yes."

"What if we left?" the older woman asked. "What if we picked up and moved?" She glanced at her husband. "We could get out of the state, at least. Try to start over somewhere new."

"You could do that," Julian agreed. "There's no guarantee you'd be safe, but that's one approach."

"I don't want to move."

Everyone turned at the sound of the new voice. Ruth twisted around in her seat to see Lily standing in the doorway to the formal dining room.

"Lily," Margaret chided. "You're supposed to be doing your homework."

"This is more interesting," she said, stepping into the room.

"How long have you been listening?" George asked. He sounded defeated, as though he knew there was no point in scolding the girl.

"Long enough," Lily said. She stood next to Julian. "So they want to kill me now?"

Julian turned and gave Ruth a panicked look. Under any other circumstances, she would have laughed to see him so flustered. "Um, well," he began.

"I found a threatening note in my office," Ruth said, deciding to spare him. "We think it's from the same people who killed your parents. They appear to be worried about what you've been telling me and the police."

"So they want me to stop talking," Lily said.

Ruth nodded. "Your grandparents are worried, and rightly so."

Lily glanced at them, her expression softening. "I know."

"Sweetheart, I think you'd better get back to your homework," Margaret suggested.

"I will," Lily replied. "But I want to know what's going to happen first."

"Nothing's going to happen," George said. "We're going to keep you safe. Don't worry about that."

Lily fixed her gaze on Julian. "What did the note say?"

Julian hesitated. "It said you need to stop talking," he paraphrased.

"Or else?" she guessed.

Julian nodded. "Basically."

Ruth breathed a silent sigh of relief, grateful he hadn't shared the exact wording of the threat.

"But you want me to keep going." She wasn't asking; Lily appeared to be looking for a confirmation of what she already knew.

"I do," Julian said simply. "I think it's our best chance of drawing these guys out into the open and arresting them."

Lily studied him for a moment, then looked at Ruth. "What do you think?"

Ruth took a deep breath. She was still uncertain of the right choice, but Lily deserved an answer and based on her behavior, Ruth had a good idea of what she wanted to do. Maybe this was the sign she'd prayed for?

"I think he's right. But," she added quickly, "I also think you've done so much for the police already. If you're scared to keep going, no one would blame you." She knew what it felt like to want to fight for justice for a loved one. But Lily was so young, and her situation was so dangerous…

"Wait a minute," George interjected. "There's no debate here. We already said no."

Lily didn't respond to her grandfather's protest. She held Ruth's gaze, as if trying to see into her soul.

Ruth didn't flinch. She looked into the girl's blue eyes, trying to silently convey her unconditional support for whatever Lily decided to do.

She wasn't sure how much time passed. Everyone else in the room seemed to hold their breath, until at last, Lily nodded.

"All right," she declared. "I'll do it."

"Lily," said Margaret, speaking at the same time as George, who burst out with, "I forbid it."

Lily turned to look at her grandparents. "I want to try," she said calmly.

"You don't understand the risks!" George exclaimed. "I can't let you volunteer for something like this."

"We're just trying to keep you safe," Margaret pleaded. "We won't allow you to antagonize these people."

"This is our best chance," Lily said. She glanced at Julian, then back to her family. "Don't you see? This is our best chance to catch the people who killed Mom and Dad. Don't you want that?"

"Of course we do," George said. "But not if it means risking your safety."

"You have to let me try." There was an edge to Lily's voice now and something shifted in the air. She was no longer asking; she was telling. "I need to do this."

"There has to be another way," Margaret suggested. But Lily shook her head.

"No. This is it."

"The answer is no, Lily," George said firmly. "And that's final."

Lily stared at her grandfather for a minute. "Fine." Her flat voice sent a chill skittering down Ruth's spine; it was the same tone she'd had when they'd first started their sessions together. "I'll just wait until you're asleep and then run away."

Ruth sucked in a breath as the color drained from George's face. "Don't even joke about that," he said.

"I'm not kidding," Lily said. She jerked a thumb in Julian's direction. "He's trying to catch the people who did this. I'm going to help him."

Ruth felt like she had to intervene before the conversation spiraled out of control. "Lily, I know you're eager to help. But there are other ways to do it."

The young girl shook her head. "He said it himself." She gestured to Julian again. "Even if I stop talking to you guys, they're still going to come after us. So why is it better for me to hide?"

"It's not," Margaret said miserably. She leaned over and placed her hand on George's arm. "If we do this, there's a greater chance the killers will be found. If we hide, we'll be looking over our shoulders for the rest of our lives."

"And if they aren't arrested?" George asked.

"Then nothing changes," Julian said quietly. "But at least you'll know you tried everything."

"Even if it costs us everything?" George shot back.

Julian didn't reply. Silence fell over the room, the atmosphere still thick with tension.

Lily quietly walked over to her grandfather and wrapped her arms around his shoulders. "Please," she said softly.

George embraced his granddaughter, his internal struggle playing out on his face. "All right," he choked out, his eyes shining with unshed tears. "I can see I've been outvoted. Two against one."

Margaret gave him an understanding smile. Ruth glanced at Julian, wondering if he too felt like an intruder on this personal moment.

He cleared his throat. "I'll be in touch soon to give you more details about your protection at home and the measures we'll put into place to guard Lily while she's at school or meeting with Ruth."

George nodded. "Fine."

"In the meantime," Julian continued, "I'll have a squad car stationed here twenty-four seven. You might see them change shifts every few hours, but you don't need to worry."

"Thank you," Margaret said.

Ruth pushed back from the table, and Julian stood, as well. "Thank you for speaking with us," she said.

George nodded silently, but he shook Julian's hand. Ruth hugged Margaret, then turned to embrace Lily.

"Go easy on them," she whispered in the girl's ear.

Lily nodded. "I wasn't really going to run away," she whispered back.

Ruth shook her head slightly as she looked down at Lily. Part of her was pleased to see Lily standing up for what she wanted. The girl who'd started therapy nine months ago had been scared of her own shadow, but now here she was, determined to help Julian catch the men who had killed her parents. It was quite a transformation, and brought back memories of her own family's fight for justice for her sister.

She and Julian finished saying their goodbyes, then stepped outside. He walked over to the squad car and exchanged a few words with the officers inside, then unlocked his truck and helped her into the passenger seat.

She waited for him to climb behind the wheel before talking. "That went well, all things considered."

He nodded. "I think so, too."

"So what happens now?" Lily's next appointment wasn't for another week. Were they supposed to just sit around and wait until then?

A look of determination crossed Julian's face. "Now we find out more about Eric."

Ruth had filled him in on the name in Lily's journal on the way over to the Pushkins'. She knew he'd wanted to ask Lily a few questions about it, but it was clear the family needed time to themselves first to process this new development.

Julian fished his cell phone out of his pocket. "Do me a favor?" he asked, tossing it into her lap.

"Sure."

He nodded at the phone. "Text Sam." He reached over and used his fingerprint to unlock the device.

"What do you want me to say?" Ruth asked.

"Just the name Eric," he said. "Add a question mark at the end."

Ruth typed the message and held the screen up so

Julian could read it. It couldn't be more basic, but she didn't want to risk getting anything wrong.

"Perfect," Julian said. "Send it, please."

She did as he asked, then set the phone on the console between their seats. "Think he'll answer you?"

Julian shook his head. "I don't know. But it's as good a place as any to start." He tapped a beat onto the steering wheel. "You hungry?"

Her heart leaped at the question and its implication. More time with Julian? Yes, please.

"I'm getting there," she said, trying not to sound too eager.

He smiled at her. "Me, too. Want to grab a bite?"

Ruth nodded, feeling an answering grin tugging at the corners of her mouth. "Absolutely."

Ruth rolled onto her back and stared at the shadows on the ceiling of her room, her mind too busy for sleep.

Dinner with Julian had been…very nice. She smiled as she recalled their conversation, remembering the easy banter they'd fallen into after sitting down at the restaurant. Normally, Ruth was aware of the time, as she hated being late to anything. But when she was with Julian, she never checked her watch. It was easy to forget about the rest of the world when he was around. Those dark brown eyes of his were nearly intoxicating, drawing Ruth in until the world shrank to just the two of them.

Their conversation tonight hadn't all been lighthearted fun, though. Julian was worried about her living alone.

"You might be a target, too," he'd pointed out.

The thought had scared Ruth—even now, the idea

that someone could be lurking outside her home made her a little nauseous. But she wasn't going to upend her entire life just because there was a chance that someone, somewhere *might* be upset with her. She refused to live in fear, even if that fear was possibly justified.

She'd said as much to Julian, though she could tell from his frown that he wasn't impressed with her determination to carry on as though things were normal. He'd wanted to post a squad car at her curb, just as he'd done for the Pushkins. That had seemed like a waste of police time and resources, so Ruth had turned him down. Undeterred, Julian had told her he'd make sure the police drove by her house several times tonight, just in case. And after dinner, he'd followed her home to make sure no one was lying in wait in her closet.

It had felt strange having Julian in her space. He hadn't stayed very long; he'd simply done a quick search of the place to double-check that she was alone and all her doors and windows were locked. Even though he'd left hours ago, the memory of him lingered in her rooms. She'd never invited a man into her home before—at least, not a man she was romantically interested in. Just being near him had been enough to make her head spin pleasantly. It was yet another sign that her attraction to him was building at a record pace.

Julian had hugged her goodbye, making her promise to sleep with her cell phone next to her pillow. Ruth had rolled her eyes but agreed. And she'd kept her word— the phone sat on her bedside table, on top of her journal. She was tempted to pick it up and call Julian now so they could keep talking. The idea of falling asleep with his voice in her ear was deeply appealing. But Ruth knew he needed his sleep. Just because she was awake didn't mean he had to be, as well. Besides, if she called him at this hour, he'd worry something was wrong. Not exactly the makings of a romantic conversation.

She turned onto her side with a sigh. What was she doing? She'd never been this drawn to a man before. But it wasn't just her hormones talking. She felt as though Julian really saw her. Like he recognized who she was and understood what she wanted out of life. The more she learned about him, the more she felt like they just clicked. It was a novel experience, and she was enjoying every minute of it.

But she couldn't silence the chiding voice in her head that told her she had no business pursuing a personal relationship while poor Lily was going through so much. The girl was dealing with her memories of that horrible night, and now she and her grandparents were facing new threats. On some level, it felt wrong that Ruth was enjoying herself and finding happiness in the midst of these circumstances.

I don't know what to do. Should she give up seeing Julian in favor of helping Lily? Or should she take the chance she'd been given and see how things developed between them? Was there a way for her to do both? Could she still support Lily and her grandparents and develop a relationship with Julian? Ruth felt like there was room in her life for both options, but was she simply being selfish? The last thing she wanted was to hurt Lily, but the more she got to know Julian, the more she cared about him, as well.

Despite her growing feelings for Julian, a kernel of doubt persisted. What if she was making a mistake?

She'd seen firsthand how Julian could throw up a wall between them and cut her off; sure, he was open and caring now, but what if something happened and things changed? She'd wind up hurt and possibly nursing a broken heart.

There was also the matter of his job. As a police officer, he faced danger regularly. She knew he was upset over the gang's threats, but not because he was worried about himself—his concern was all for her and Lily. Julian wasn't reckless, but she didn't understand how he was able to stay so calm and levelheaded in the face of such darkness. Could she really be with him, knowing he could be taken from her without warning, just like Mary?

Ruth closed her eyes and began to pray, asking for direction. Her worries calmed as she gave them over to God, trusting that she would receive the guidance she needed. A sense of peace washed over her, and as she finished praying, she felt once more that everything would be okay. It was the same sensation she'd had in her office, after talking to Julian this afternoon. She'd been so stressed about the note, worried about Lily and the case. So while Julian had taken photos of her desk, Ruth had silently prayed for help. Within minutes, her worries had calmed, as though the storm had blown out to sea. As far as signs went, it was a pretty clear one.

Ruth didn't know what the future held for her and Julian. But the more time she spent with him, the more convinced she became that this was an opportunity she couldn't pass up. That family and the children she'd been dreaming about weren't going to happen if she never found someone to share her life with. She owed it to herself to discover if Julian was that man.

Ruth came awake with a start as the mattress shifted under her. In the split second after opening her eyes, she saw a large, menacing shadow at the end of her bed. Her heart jumped into her throat and she let out a strangled scream as she sat up and tried to scramble out from under the covers. But her legs were tangled in the sheets, and the weight of the person at the end of her bed pinned her under the blankets.

A hand clamped around her wrist. "I'm not here to hurt you."

The man's gruff voice cut through her panic, though she didn't believe him. He held on to her arm even as she pushed herself up the bed, trying to put distance between them. Her back hit the headboard and she glanced to her bedside table. Could she reach the lamp with her free arm? She stretched, her fingers almost brushing the surface…

"Don't," he said shortly. His grip tightened on her arm in warning. She let her hand drop, but continued trying to inch off the bed. *Please no, please no, please no…* The words rattled in her brain on repeat, keeping time with her pounding heart.

"I just need you to listen." He leaned forward, coming closer. Her chest tightened as he loomed over her. She instinctively angled her body to the side to avoid touching him.

"Look at me." There was an urgency in his voice, a note of desperation that made her turn back. He sounded almost scared, but that couldn't be it. He'd broken into her home. He was sitting on her bed, waking her up in the middle of the night. Why should he be afraid?

But as the seconds ticked by, Ruth's initial panic started to calm and her thoughts came back online. Whoever this man was, he hadn't hurt her. Not yet, anyway. He still held her wrist, but his grip was loose, not painful. And that was their only point of contact—he hadn't tried to touch her anywhere else.

Ruth slowly turned her head to face him again. He leaned forward a bit, just enough to put his face in the soft beam of moonlight streaming in from her window. As soon as she saw him, recognition slammed into her.

"It's you." The man Julian had spoken to outside the restaurant. The undercover cop. What was his name?

He nodded and released her wrist, then scooted back down the mattress. "Yeah. It's me."

"Sam," she said, dredging up his name from her memory. "How did you get in? Julian isn't here."

"I picked the lock on your door." He stood and walked over to the chair in the corner of her room. "And I know you're alone. That's the point. I'm here to talk to you."

Ruth felt her jaw drop. "And you thought this was the best way to do that?" She reached for the edge of the sheet, pulling it up over her body. Having a strange man in her room made her feel exposed and vulnerable.

"I'm sorry." There was genuine remorse in his voice, but it still didn't excuse his actions. "I know it seems extreme, but breaking in like this is the safest way for me to see you."

"Why's that?" Ruth's temper was quickly burning through her initial fear. How dare he invade her space and terrorize her in the middle of the night! She grabbed the cell phone off the bedside table and clutched it to her chest. The logical part of her realized that Julian couldn't just materialize here to help her, but knowing she could call him made her feel marginally better.

"The note in your office today—" he began.

"That was you," she interrupted, her tone sharp.

"Yeah." She couldn't see his face in the shadows, but she saw him nod. "I had to."

"So you're the gang's messenger boy?" *What are you doing?* she asked herself. Cop or no, taunting Sam was not the smartest idea. She was alone in her bedroom with him, and while Julian seemed to think he was a good guy, he was still a gang member. Julian himself had said he thought the experience had changed Sam. She thought back to Julian's description of gang initiations. What had they asked Sam to do before accepting him? Goose bumps broke out over her body as her imagination ran wild.

His voice cut through her thoughts. "I am," he confirmed. If he was bothered by her sarcasm, he didn't show it. "You need to watch yourself."

"Why am I a target?" Ruth asked. Her teeth ground together as she clenched her jaw in frustration. "I don't know anything."

Sam scoffed. "We both know that's not true. Let's not waste each other's time."

Ruth swallowed hard as her stomach churned. "Are you here to kill me?"

"No," he said. "I'm not supposed to be here at all."

"Then why—"

"You have a target on your back, Ms. Becker. The

gang leadership knows Lily Pushkin is remembering details about that night. They know about the sketch. And they're not pleased."

"How is that possible?" Her thoughts whirled as she considered different scenarios. As far as she knew, Sam was the only person other than police who had seen the sketch. So that must mean… "Did you show them?" Was he playing both sides? Trying to cover all the bases to keep himself safe, no matter the outcome?

"It didn't come from me," he said.

Of course he'd say that. He'd be a bad double agent if he admitted to betraying the police at the first question of his loyalty. But what if he was telling the truth? Julian seemed to think Sam was fundamentally a good guy. Maybe he wasn't lying? That meant the leak must have come from within the police department.

"I don't know who it was," Sam said, as though he'd read her mind. "But someone is feeding information to the gang."

"Can't you find out?" Ruth asked. "You're in a unique position to figure out who's helping the gang."

"Not really," Sam said. "Only a few people know I'm undercover. If I start poking around too much, it'll raise suspicions and that will cause problems."

"They're threatening to murder a child," Ruth said. "Isn't that worth more than your position?"

"It's not up to me," Sam replied, an edge to his voice. "Of course I don't want to see anything happen to her. Or you, either. Why do you think I'm here?"

"I don't know!" Exasperation built in her chest, making her voice loud. "You haven't told me anything I didn't already know from the note you delivered to my office."

"I'm trying to warn you," Sam said. "You need to get out. Stop meeting with Lily. Stop trying to help Julian. You're not part of this. If you quit now, you'll probably be okay. But if you keep going, you're going to get lumped in with Lily and Julian."

The hairs on the back of Ruth's neck rose. "So Julian is in danger, too?"

"Yeah," Sam confirmed. "Everyone who is part of this case has a target on their back."

"Why are you involved?" Ruth asked. "Julian told me you were getting initiated when the Pushkins were murdered. Why are you so wrapped up in this now?"

Sam didn't reply. But he didn't need to. The answer came to her in the silence.

"Because you're the man in the sketch." She shook her head, the pieces falling into place. "There was no other recruit who looked like you. You were the one who was there that night."

Sam still didn't speak. "Why did you lie to Julian?" she asked.

"He's always been a straight shooter," Sam said finally. "He's always been honest, almost to a fault. I knew him a little, before I graduated. The police academy taught us that sometimes you have to bend the truth a little when you're questioning a suspect. Sometimes you have to make them think you know things that you don't, to get them to confess. But Julian never would. He was determined that he could do the job without lying. Probably because of his dad."

Ruth's curiosity woke up at that. "What about his

dad?" On some level, she knew she shouldn't be talking about this with Sam. If she wanted to know about Julian's family, she should ask him. But he hadn't shared much about them, except to say that his father had died a few years ago.

"Julian's father was a cop on the take in Phoenix," Sam replied. "The family had no idea until he was indicted. It was just as Julian was starting the academy."

Ruth leaned back against the headboard, her heart aching for Julian. She knew all too well what it felt like to be betrayed by the police. But it must have been so much worse for him, knowing his own father was guilty.

"I've always admired Julian," Sam went on. "If he knows the truth…"

"So you're trying to protect yourself."

Sam leaned forward. "I hate myself for what happened. It's haunted me for years."

"Good," Ruth shot back. She didn't feel sorry for him, wasn't going to try to absolve him of his guilt. "It should. You destroyed a family that night."

"I didn't kill anyone!" She saw his fist clench in the moonlight and tensed. Was he going to attack her?

"You stood by and did nothing," she said quietly. "Isn't that the same thing?"

"You don't understand." She heard the anguish in Sam's voice, but she couldn't offer him comfort. "The Pushkins weren't supposed to die. I was told we were sent there to deliver a message, to scare him off. But things got out of hand, and the guy I was with—"

"Eric?" Ruth supplied.

His head snapped up. "How did you know that?" He

waved a hand in a dismissive gesture. "Never mind. Yeah, Eric was a little too trigger-happy."

"So he shot Lily's parents?"

Sam nodded. "I saw Lily down the hall. She'd opened her bedroom door when the shouting started. At least Eric had his back to her room, and I tried to keep it that way. I watched her crawl under the bed and hide. Eric wanted to search her room after, but I told him we had to get out of there. So we left."

"Why didn't you try to stop him?"

"It all happened so fast," Sam said. "By the time I realized what he was doing, it was over."

"But what about after?" she asked. "Maybe you couldn't have stopped him, but why didn't you arrest him later?"

She shrank back as Sam shot to his feet and began to pace by the foot of her bed. "I wanted to. I told my handler as soon as I got a moment to myself. He reported it up the chain of command, but they ultimately told me to stand down."

"I don't understand," Ruth said. "Why wouldn't they want you to arrest a murderer?"

"They said my position in the gang was too important. Phoenix PD had spent years trying to get into the gang. I was the first one to make it. If I arrested Eric, or even if someone else arrested him, they would know the information came from me."

"So they put your job over the lives of Lily's parents." Disgust filled her, and the face of the officer who had killed her sister came to mind. She saw it all again, the cop and his buddies celebrating in the courtroom after the judge's ruling.

"It wasn't just Phoenix PD," Sam said. "The Feds were involved, as well. ATF, FBI, Homeland Security... Everyone was excited to have someone on the inside with the Rising Suns. They're making a name for themselves, not just in Arizona, but throughout the Southwest. A lot of law enforcement agencies are trying to bring them down. In the end, someone decided that justice for the Pushkins would have to wait."

"And you were okay with that?"

"No," Sam said quietly. "But what choice did I have? If I disobeyed orders and made an arrest, I would have burned my bridges with the police and they wouldn't have protected me. The gang would have realized who I was and tortured and killed me. If I'd just quit the force, I'd still have to deal with the gang. No one gets out of the Rising Suns alive. By staying in, I have at least a bit of protection if things go sideways."

"What, like witness protection?" Ruth didn't understand how Sam could trust the police at all. If they'd throw him to the wolves for doing his job, what made him think they would help him if the gang turned on him later?

He stopped and shrugged. "It's better than nothing."

"What about now?" she challenged. "Are the people in charge still willing to look the other way, now that a child and a cop are being threatened?" *Not to mention me*, she added silently.

"I don't know," he said with a sigh. "They might decide to just let things play out, rather than step in and expose the fact that there's a mole in the gang. If the police or Feds act to prevent retaliation against you or

Lily or Julian, it will tip off the fact that we've infiltrated the Rising Suns."

"Well, we wouldn't want that." Ruth didn't bother
to hide her sarcasm.

"I know it's not fair or right," Sam said. "Believe
me, I'm trying my best on both sides to keep things
from escalating. I don't want any more deaths on my
conscience."

"Is that why you're here?" she asked. "To ease your
guilt?"

"Partly," Sam admitted. "I was hoping you'd go away
after I warned you. But you aren't going to, are you?"
He sounded a little sad, as though she was disappoint-
ing him.

"I can't," she replied. "I care about Lily and Julian.
I won't stand by and watch while they risk their own
safety to do the right thing."

"You're a good match for him," Sam said. "I think
he'll listen to you. So tell him to stop contacting me.
It's not safe for either one of us."

"I'll try," she said. "But he's worried about you."

Sam laughed softly. "That'll change. Once you tell
him what I told you, he'll never look at me the same
way again."

Ruth considered his words. "Actually, I think you
should be the one to tell him about your role that night."

"Why would I do that?"

"It's not my story," Ruth said, anger making her voice
cold. "I can't give you absolution for what you've done.
Even if I told you I understood your actions, it wouldn't
matter because you don't know me. That has to come
from your friend. And unless you step up and tell him

yourself, you don't have a chance of earning his forgiveness."

Sam was silent for a moment. Finally, he let out a sigh. "I know."

"You say that night has haunted you. If you really want to unburden yourself, talk to Julian."

"Maybe I will." He headed for her bedroom door, then paused. "Eric's in prison. He won't be hard to find. But he's got connections. I don't know who they are, but he has powerful friends. Tell Julian to tread lightly."

"Sam?"

"Yeah?"

Ruth swallowed hard, her throat suddenly dry. "If they come for me...for us... Can you at least make sure it'll be quick?"

He made a pained sound low in his throat, then turned and walked out of the room without saying another word.

Ruth waited until she heard her front door snick shut. Then she ran down the hallway, flipped the lock back into place and dragged a chair in front of the door.

At that point, her strength drained away and she dropped to the ground. She drew her knees up to her chest and wrapped her arms around her legs, hugging herself.

She had to talk to Julian. Had to warn him that he was a target, too. She'd thought he was overreacting when he'd tried to assign a squad car to her home, but after Sam's visit, she was ready to turn her house into Fort Knox.

Eventually, she felt like she could stand again. Ruth got to her feet, her legs still feeling shaky. She made her way back to her bedroom, running a hand along the wall to steady herself. The phone was next to her bed, where it had fallen when she'd run out of the room.

She crawled back into bed, trying to decide what to do next. Sam had come here to warn her, which meant the gang wasn't ready to attack just yet. And if they weren't ready to hurt her, they probably weren't ready to hurt Julian yet, either. Lily's house was guarded by the police, so they should be safe. But should she call Julian now and wake him up? Or was it better to let him sleep and tell him in the morning?

After debating for several minutes, Ruth decided to wait until tomorrow. If she called him now, Julian would insist on coming over to make sure she was safe. Since there wasn't anything he could do at this point, she shouldn't interrupt his night. Maybe she'd even fall asleep again, though that seemed unlikely given the fact her heart was still pounding and she felt shaky from adrenaline. Still, there was no point in both of them being tired tomorrow.

Ruth curled up on the bed, clutching the phone to her chest. A snippet of a church song drifted through her mind, and she latched on like a lifeline. She started humming to herself, using her phone to play one song after another. As long as she was thinking about music, she wasn't thinking about the gang, the Pushkin murders and the fact that she was now a target.

Eventually, Ruth closed her eyes, the music helping her relax. Soon she was slipping into sleep, the songs of her childhood echoing in her ears.

Chapter Eight

Julian had just finished talking to the warden at the state prison in Tucson when his cell phone buzzed with a text. He glanced at the screen and smiled when he saw Ruth's name.

Are you free?

He typed in a response: I can be. What's up?

Her reply was almost instantaneous. Meet me at the café across from the police station.

Julian lifted one eyebrow as he read her message, his curiosity growing. This seemed a little cloak-and-dagger, especially for Ruth. She was normally straightforward and to the point. So why didn't she want to meet him at his desk? Or have him come to her office?

He stood up and slipped on a sport coat to cover his shoulder holster. Then he walked out the front doors of the station and crossed the street. He was familiar with the café she'd suggested; he often stopped here for coffee in the morning when he had time.

Ruth was already there, waiting for him at a table in the corner. For a split second, Julian had a sense of déjà vu. Hadn't they met like this only a few days ago? A different place, but still… Shaking off the odd sensation, Julian walked over to her table.

"Hey." He smiled at her as he took the seat across from her. Ruth smiled back, but it seemed slightly forced. He noted the dark circles under her eyes and the strain lines at the corners of her mouth. She gripped a paper napkin in her hands, her fingers clenched so tightly she was tearing it.

A sense of uneasiness began to stir in Julian's stomach. "What's going on?" he asked. "Did you get any sleep last night?"

Ruth shook her head. "Not much. I had a visitor."

That got his attention. Julian's unease turned to alarm and he leaned in, scanning her for any signs of injury. "What do you mean? Are you okay?" He heard the sharpness in his voice but didn't care. He silently kicked himself for not insisting on posting an officer at her house last night. She'd talked him out of it, saying it wasn't necessary. But it sounded like she'd been wrong.

Ruth held up a hand and glanced to the side. Julian followed her gaze and realized the couple a few tables over was looking at them. Apparently, he'd been a little too loud.

Adjusting the volume of his voice, Julian spoke again. "What happened? Why didn't you call me?" Anger flared in his chest as he looked at her, wondering why she hadn't reached out. Did she not think he was capable of protecting her?

"I'm fine. There wasn't anything you could have done."

"Oh yeah?" There was a lot he could have done, starting with posting a guard at her door and ending with him arresting whoever had dared break into her place. Just the thought of someone invading her space made him see red.

"Julian," she pleaded.

He took a deep breath and forced himself to relax. They could talk about her lack of trust in him later. She did appear to be fine, but he still didn't like the thought of someone threatening her while she was alone. "Just tell me what happened, please."

"I'm trying to." Exasperation flitted across her face. "Sam came to see me last night."

Julian shook his head, certain he'd misunderstood. "I'm sorry, did you say Sam?"

She nodded as she wrapped her hands around her mug of tea. "Yes. Scared me to death, too. I woke up from a sound sleep to find him sitting at the foot of my bed. I thought he was an intruder." She tilted her head to the side. "I mean, he was an intruder, in a way. But he wasn't there to hurt me."

Julian was still stuck on the fact that Sam had broken into her home. "What did he want?"

"To warn me. He said if I kept meeting with Lily I would be in danger just like the two of you."

"The two of us?" Julian repeated. "So I'm on their radar, as well?"

Ruth nodded. "He said the gang was unhappy the case is being reopened. That the three of us needed to stop, or else."

"I see." He leaned back, processing this information. In some ways, Julian was used to being in danger. It was part of the job description, to a certain extent. But he'd never before been personally targeted due to his actions. It felt a little strange, disturbing even.

But something wasn't adding up. "Did he tell you how the gang knows the case has been reopened? I just assumed they had people watching Lily, but is there more to it than that?"

Ruth cast a furtive glance around. "That's why I wanted to meet you here. Sam told me the gang knows about it because someone is feeding them information."

Julian sucked in a breath. "You mean a cop?"

Ruth nodded. "I think so."

His mind started to race. "I don't suppose he told you who?"

She shook her head. "He said he couldn't poke around too much or it would raise suspicion." She leaned forward and lowered her voice. "Here's the thing. Sam knew about the sketch because you told him. I assume other people in your department know about it, too?"

Julian nodded, wondering where she was going with this. He'd shown the drawing to a few people, but only those who had some kind of connection to the case. He hadn't posted it to the bulletin board or anything.

"He told me the gang leadership had heard about the sketch and they were upset. I asked Sam if he was the one talking to them, and he denied it. I don't know if he's telling the truth, but if he's being honest, it means someone else is their source."

Julian's initial shock was quickly giving way to anger. He considered the people he'd spoken to about the case, evaluating their conversations in a new light. Which one of them had shared their knowledge with the gang? Who would betray him like that?

Memories of his father bubbled to the surface. His dad had seemed like a stand-up guy, the type of person who would never do anything wrong. But that had turned out to be a lie. And now it looked like one of his coworkers was two-faced, as well.

"Julian." Ruth's voice cut through his thoughts. He focused on her face and found her watching him, looking worried. "I don't know if you can trust Sam. Remember how you told me going through the initiation and being a gang member might have changed him?"

He nodded. "You think he's lying?"

"I think you have to consider the possibility that he might be, yes," she said carefully.

Julian frowned. "Why do I get the feeling there's something you're not telling me?"

Something flashed in her eyes, there and gone so quickly he couldn't identify the emotion. "I'm just saying, I think you should be careful with what you tell him."

She was definitely holding something back, but Julian sensed that if he tried to pry, she'd shut down. So he changed tactics. "Did he tell you anything else?"

Ruth glanced away, an uncharacteristically evasive move that made his curiosity flare. Sam had done more than warn her about the gang, that was certain. But what? Had he hurt her in some way? Maybe done things Ruth didn't want to talk about? A chill skittered down his spine, and he bit his tongue to keep from pressing for more information. If something had happened—and that was a big if—then he didn't want to make things harder for her by needling her for details.

Still, her apparent reluctance to confide in him stung. Maybe she didn't trust him as much as he hoped? He'd thought they were connecting well, but perhaps he was mistaken?

Ruth's words brought him back to the issue at hand. "He said Eric was in prison and would be easy to find."

"I know," Julian said. "I've already found him." Was that all? No, there had to be more—that was definitely guilt he saw on her face. What could have possibly happened to make her feel guilty?

Ruth's eyes widened. "You have?"

He nodded, his earlier pleasure at the discovery dampened. "Yeah. He's at the federal prison in Tucson. I had just finished talking to the warden when you texted me."

"Are you going to talk to him?"

"That was my plan."

Ruth bit her bottom lip. "Can I come?"

Julian tilted his head to the side, surprised by her interest. "Sure. I would have invited you, but I figured you had to work."

She shook her head. "I've cleared my schedule for the next few days."

"I see." He leaned forward and took one of her hands, holding it between his own. "Ruth, I'm going to be honest with you. I can tell that something is bothering you. I know it must have been terrifying for you to wake up and find Sam in your home, but if he did anything more than talk to you, I want you to know you can tell me. I can help you."

She regarded him with a puzzled expression for a second, but then realization dawned. "Oh," she said. "No, nothing like that happened." She shook her head firmly. "I appreciate your willingness to help, but he really didn't touch me."

He was relieved to hear it, but he couldn't shake the feeling there was more she wasn't telling him. "Did he say something to upset you?"

"You mean besides the stuff about the gang wanting to kill me if I don't back down?" Her tone was artificially light, underscoring the absurdity of his question.

He nodded. "Well, yeah. Other than that."

Ruth pressed her lips together, then sighed. "He told me a little about your father."

Julian leaned back, releasing her hand. "What did he say?"

She looked pained. "That your dad was a police officer in Phoenix. That he was indicted just after you'd started the academy."

"I see." A chill began in his chest and spread throughout his body, making him feel numb. He hadn't wanted Ruth to know about his father. Not yet, anyway. Given her history with police corruption, he hadn't figured out the best way to talk to her about his dad. If he was being completely honest with himself, he still didn't know the best way to think about his dad. But he did know this—Sam had no right to tell Ruth such personal details.

"I'm sorry," she said. She reached across the table for his hand, but he barely registered her touch. "I wish he hadn't told me. But I figured you should know that I know."

"And what do you think?" He braced himself for her reply. It wasn't that long ago that she'd accused him of protecting Sam at the expense of Lily. He'd managed to convince her he wasn't trying to cover up any wrongdoing, but would this new information change her opinion of him? Would she be less likely to give him the benefit of the doubt now that she knew his father had been a liar and a criminal? After all, the apple didn't fall far from the tree. At least, that was what some people thought.

"I don't have all the details," she said. "But based on what I know about you, I'm sure that was a very hard time for you and your family."

Julian bit back the sarcastic response that immediately sprang to his lips. Ruth didn't deserve his defensiveness. "It was," he said instead. He briefly considered telling her about the last conversation he'd had with his father, but decided against it. He wanted to stay focused on this case, not relitigate the past.

"Is that why you work so hard?" she asked quietly. "Because you're trying to prove you're different?"

He looked at the table, at their joined hands. Hers were so delicate—her palms narrow, her fingers long. Her wrists looked small and fragile compared to his, her skin pale against his darker color.

It felt strange, being the recipient of someone's solace. Usually Julian was the one trying to make others feel better. He couldn't remember the last time a woman had tried to comfort him, aside from his mother. Those he'd dated in the past had never seemed to realize that even though he kept his emotions locked down, he still needed someone to check on him, too, to make sure he was okay.

Part of that had undoubtedly been his fault—he wasn't very good at being vulnerable in a relationship, so he'd never really been able to click with anyone. But there was something about Ruth that made him feel safe, made him think he could let down his guard and talk to her, and she wouldn't judge him. It scared him a little, the idea of sharing so much with her. But it was also deeply appealing. He'd been carrying the burden of his father's death for so long; it would feel good to set it down, if only for a short time.

When this is over, he thought to himself. Once the Pushkin case was solved and the threats from the gang were behind them, Julian would talk to Ruth. But he couldn't afford to take the time for a heart-to-heart now.

"That's partially why," he said, knowing he needed to answer her question. "Some people have judged me for his actions. I guess I want them to know we're different people."

Ruth squeezed his hand. "I understand."

"We should probably get going," he said, changing the subject. "The warden said I could talk to Eric in a couple of hours, and by the time we get to Tucson and get checked in at the prison, he should be ready."

A shadow crossed Ruth's face. "Julian, Sam said one more thing before he left last night. He told me Eric has connections, and you need to be careful."

Julian frowned. "I appreciate the warning, but I'm not going to just sit behind my desk now that I have a new lead. If what Sam says is true, this is the man who killed Lily's parents. I'm not going to pass up an opportunity to talk to him just because it will make some gang members angry."

"I know," Ruth said, shaking her head. "I figured you would ignore the warning."

"But you don't have to," he replied. "You don't have to come with me. There's no sense in making the target on your back any bigger."

Ruth met his eyes, determination shining in her gaze. "I'm going," she said. "I won't leave you to do this by yourself. Not if there's any way I can help."

Julian nodded, a little relieved by her declaration. He didn't like the idea of Ruth being alone, especially after her nocturnal visit from Sam. She might not be willing to call him for help in the middle of the night, but if she came with him, at least he'd be able to keep her safe while they were together. And he could spend the drive to Tucson convincing her to let him assign some officers to her home. It was a win-win, as far as he was concerned.

The fact that he now had an excuse to spend more time with her, one-on-one, during a workday no less? That was simply the icing on the cake.

Traffic was light, so the drive to Tucson didn't take very long. Ruth wouldn't have minded a longer trip; it was nice to just be with Julian, without any interruptions.

They spent the time talking. He told her about his experiment with music the other day, and how listening to Mozart had helped change his mood. Ruth was delighted to hear it—she got the impression that before meeting her, Julian would have never considered trying music as a way to handle his emotions. Maybe she was rubbing off on him?

They were still chatting when his phone rang. He gave her an apologetic look. "Sorry, I should take this."

"Of course." Just because she had cleared her schedule didn't mean he could say the same.

He pressed a button, and a voice filled the truck. "Detective Aguirre?"

"That's me."

"This is Judy Garber with Winthrop and Daniels. I received your message about wanting access to Gregory Pushkin's case files?"

"Yes, that's correct. I'm investigating his murder and I was hoping to examine the cases he was working on prior to his death."

There was a pause on the other end of the line. "I wasn't aware the case was still active."

"There's no statute of limitations on murder," Julian said easily. "And some new evidence has come to light."

"Ah," said Judy. "That's good to hear. However, I can't just hand over Mr. Pushkin's files. After his death, his cases were reassigned to our other attorneys. The files contain privileged information."

"I understand, but—"

"As such, Detective, I'm afraid I cannot grant you access to those files."

Julian's hands tightened on the steering wheel. *He's getting frustrated*, Ruth thought. Not that she blamed him—Judy wasn't exactly being helpful. "Is the list of his clients at the time of his death privileged information?" he asked.

"No, but—" Judy sounded reluctant, as though she didn't want to answer his question.

"Then I'd appreciate you sending me a list of the

cases he was working on by the end of the day," Julian said. "Otherwise, the next time I contact you, it will be with a court order in hand."

"I'll pass your request along to Mr. Winthrop," she said.

"Excellent," Julian replied. "I know Winthrop and Daniels has a good reputation. I'm sure they want to avoid any hint of interfering with a high-profile murder investigation."

Ruth smiled, glad to hear Julian sticking up for himself.

"Quite," Judy said shortly. "We'll be in touch."

The line went dead and the radio returned. "Well," Ruth said. "She seems nice."

Julian laughed. "She's just doing her job. I knew the firm wasn't going to give me access to Pushkin's files, but I figured it wouldn't hurt to ask."

"Sometimes you get the answer you want?"

He nodded. "Yeah. Gotta take my shot. Every once in a while, it works out."

"I'm surprised your partner didn't look into his cases during the initial investigation." Based on what Julian had told her about Jim, it sounded like the older man was meticulous in his work. It was hard to believe he would have overlooked this detail.

"He tried," Julian said. "But the firm stonewalled him, since all the suits were still active. Jim tried to get a court order, but by that time, everyone thought it was a home invasion gone wrong. He didn't have enough evidence to suggest premeditation, and a judge wasn't going to force the law firm to turn over files pertaining to active cases without a smoking gun."

"I see," Ruth said. "But now that the cases have all been wrapped up, it shouldn't matter as much?"

Julian shrugged. "For the most part, yes. The court decisions are a matter of public record, and I'm not looking for behind-the-scenes stuff. I just want to know what he was working on and see if I can find a motive there."

"Do you think they'll turn over the list?" The woman on the phone hadn't seemed happy with Julian's amended request. Even if her boss did agree to release the information, Ruth didn't think Judy would rush to comply.

"I imagine they will. There's no reason why they shouldn't, and I wasn't joking. If I have to take things up a notch, I will."

"I can help you go through the information," Ruth offered. "If you want," she added, realizing belatedly he might not need assistance.

Julian turned to look at her. "Yeah? That would be great, actually. But what about your work?"

"I told you, I took the next few days off," she said. "With everything going on right now, I didn't want to put my clients at risk." She didn't know what the gang was going to do, but if they decided to attack her, she didn't think they'd leave any innocent bystanders alone. She couldn't jeopardize the safety of her clients like that. And while canceling her appointments wasn't a long-term solution, it bought her some time to decide what to do next.

A shadow crossed Julian's face and he took one hand off the steering wheel, placing it on her knee. "We'll figure this out," he said, squeezing gently. "I'll make sure you're safe."

Warmth spread from his touch, up her leg and into her belly. Her skin seemed to tingle, as though a thousand tiny bubbles were tickling her. His hand was large and strong on her knee, and she wrapped her fingers around his wrist, enjoying the contact between them.

She wasn't used to these feelings—yes, she encountered handsome men and found them attractive, but with Julian it was different. He was appealing on many different levels, and the fact that he seemed to like her back made her feel special. Touching him, hugging him, brushing against him as they walked together—each interaction on its own was small, but they added up to something strong. Just the thought of kissing him made butterflies take off in her stomach.

But underneath it all, she couldn't help but wonder if things were moving too fast. Was she letting her emotions take over, when she should be thinking with her head instead of her heart?

Julian chatted as he drove. While they talked, her mind kept going back to last night, and the things Sam had told her. He'd confessed to her, in a way. And while she still believed he needed to tell Julian about his involvement in the Pushkin murders, she couldn't shake the feeling that she also needed to reveal what she knew. It was important information for Julian to have before he walked in to meet with Eric, and she owed it to Lily to tell him. A tiny sliver of her conscience protested— she had told Sam she would stay quiet—but the more she thought about it, the more she realized that keeping this particular secret would hurt too many people.

Julian took the exit for the prison, and in a matter of minutes, they were driving down a long, two-lane road that stretched into the distance. Soon enough, the prison buildings appeared, sandy-colored and almost blending into the surrounding desert. They passed a sign, and several posted notices about federal property and firearms and search protocols. Julian was going too fast for her to read them all, but she got the gist of the messages. A knot formed in her stomach as they got closer and she saw more of the complex of buildings and large, fenced-in areas. She saw a few orange-clad figures milling about behind the fences, but they weren't close enough to make out faces.

"I'm guessing this is your first time visiting a prison," Julian said as he turned into a large parking lot, set off a ways from the buildings.

"Yeah," Ruth confirmed. "Are we going to be walking past the actual prison cells?" It was a disturbing thought. She had no desire to see people caged, even though she knew they were here for a reason.

"No," Julian said. "We won't see any inmates at all. We're going to be taken to a conference room, and the guards will bring Eric inside. He'll be handcuffed, and they will secure him to the table. There's no way he'll be able to touch you, so you don't need to worry about that. He might say vulgar or crude things to try to get a reaction from you. Try not to give him the satisfaction. If he sees you're not scared, he'll move on quickly."

"Okay." She swallowed, mentally steeling herself for what was to come. When she'd volunteered to accompany Julian to the prison, she hadn't thought through what the visit would actually mean. Now that she was here, she felt nervous about the upcoming encounter. What if something happened while they were here? Would Eric try to escape? Maybe he'd arranged for another prisoner to act out, to distract the guards while he tried to run...

Julian's voice interrupted her increasingly worried thoughts. "If you have to leave the room, you can. A guard will escort you back to the main entrance, and you'll be able to wait in the lobby area." He pulled into a parking spot and turned to face her. "If you'd rather, you can just wait there the whole time. I don't want you to feel like you have to come with me."

"No, I want to," she said. "I need to see him." She wanted to watch his face as Julian asked him questions, see how he responded. And even though Julian was a tall, strong man, she didn't want him to be alone with Eric. "What's he in prison for, anyway?"

"Armed robbery," Julian said. "He's not a nice guy. But you'll be safe. I'll make sure of that."

His reassurance helped calm some of her nerves. Julian moved to turn off the truck, but Ruth put her hand on his arm, stopping him. "I need to tell you something."

"Can it wait?" His eyes flicked to the large building nearby. "It's almost time for our appointment, and we'll need to go through processing to get inside."

"It's about last night. About Sam's visit."

Julian fixed his gaze on her face and his body went still. "Okay." She felt the tension building in his muscles and dropped her hand.

"There's one more thing I didn't tell you." She took a deep breath, gathering her courage. "Sam was there the night the Pushkins were murdered. There was no second recruit who looked like him. Lily saw *him*."

Julian's expression remained carefully blank. "How do you know that?"

"Because he told me."

Julian's eyebrows shot up. "He just up and confessed to murder?"

Ruth shook her head. "He insists he didn't pull the trigger. He said Eric was the one who shot them, and that it happened too fast for him to stop it."

Julian nodded slowly. "I see. So he confessed to being an accessory to murder. Like that's better."

Sarcasm dripped from his words and it was clear he was upset. But Ruth didn't know if his anger was focused solely on Sam, or if it extended to her, as well.

"Why didn't you tell me this sooner?"

She shifted in her seat. "I didn't know how. I thought he was going to tell you himself, and I wanted to give him a chance to do that. But I realized I couldn't wait for that to happen."

Julian stared at her as if she had two heads. "You actually thought a man who did nothing to prevent a double murder was going to turn himself in?" He shook his head. "You have a lot more faith in people than I do."

She flinched, but he was right. "I'm sorry," she whispered.

"What else did he say?" Julian asked. "Any other bombshells you'd care to drop before we go in there?"

"I asked him why he didn't arrest Eric after the murders. He said he wasn't allowed to. That he told the police what had happened, but they wouldn't let him do anything about it."

"Did he say why?" Julian drummed his fingers on the steering wheel, the muscles in his jaw clenched.

Ruth nodded, wishing she had told him this earlier. "Apparently, the police and several federal agencies had been trying to get into the Rising Suns for years. He was the first one to manage it. No one wanted to risk exposing him."

"So they sacrificed the Pushkins to protect their asset," Julian said. "No wonder Jim had such a hard time."

"I'm sorry," she said again. "I should have told you sooner."

He glanced back at her, the corners of his mouth still turned down. "It's fine," he said shortly. "You told me now. But if there's anything else, I'd appreciate it if you don't keep secrets."

She shook her head. "That's it. I promise."

He studied her face for a moment. Then he reached out and tucked a strand of hair behind her ear. "I get why Sam talked to you," he said. "You have a good heart, and he took advantage of it."

"I didn't mean to make things harder for you," she said.

"It's all right. Really. You told me now, and that's what matters. I'm glad you did." He looked past her to the prison beyond. "That's going to change how I talk to Eric."

"Are you going to tell him about Sam?"

Julian shook his head. "No way. I'm not going to be the one to blow Sam's cover. I want Sam to answer for what he did. But he doesn't deserve to die."

"Do you think he will?" Ruth asked. "Answer for it,

I mean? If he told me the truth, it sounds like he tried to do the right thing when it happened but was shut down. Would he be punished now?"

"No, probably not," Julian replied. "But not all punishment comes from the law. He's got to live with what went down for the rest of his life."

"He knows," Ruth said quietly, her mind drifting back to Sam's words last night. "It haunts him."

"That's good," he mused.

Ruth frowned. It wasn't like Julian to be so casually cruel.

He saw her expression and shrugged. "I just mean if it bothers him, he's still a good guy at heart."

"I hope so," she said. "He seems like a man caught in the crossfire. I think he wants to do the right thing, but he can't make a move without someone getting hurt."

Julian nodded. "That sounds about right." He turned off the engine. "Time to get moving. The sooner we get this done, the faster we can get out of here."

Ruth climbed out of the truck and stared up at the building, taking in the barbed-wire-topped fences beyond. "Fine by me," she muttered.

Chapter Nine

The conference room was small, the square table barely wide enough for Julian and Ruth to sit side by side. He glanced at her while they waited. Her body was tense, her hands clutched together in her lap, knuckles white. Her lips were pressed together, but she seemed calm enough.

"Last chance to wait outside," he said softly. He meant what he'd said earlier—he didn't want her to go through with this if it was going to upset her. It was far too hot for her to wait in the truck, but there were a few chairs in the lobby of the visitor center.

Ruth shook her head. "No," she said shortly. "I'll be fine."

The door opened, and a guard brought in a man wearing an orange jumpsuit. Eric Martinez was shorter than Julian had expected, and he'd shaved his head since his mugshot photo. But his dark eyes still held that alert, almost predatory gleam that had been captured in the picture.

Eric looked at Julian, but quickly dismissed him in

favor of checking out Ruth. The guard secured his handcuffs to the bolt in the table, then stepped back. "Let me know if you need anything," he said, closing the door after he walked into the hall.

Eric ran his eyes over Ruth in a frank appraisal that made Julian's protective instincts flare to life. What had he been thinking, bringing an attractive woman like Ruth to a men's prison? He should have insisted she wait in the lobby. But it was too late now.

"Well, this is a treat," he said, leaning forward. Ruth didn't move; she merely held his gaze, no trace of emotion on her face.

Eric smiled. "I didn't know I was getting a conjugal visit today," he said, licking his lips.

"You aren't," Julian said, his voice gruff.

Ruth didn't speak, but from the corner of his eyes, Julian saw her fingers dig into the fabric of her pants. He had to stop this.

"I'm Detective Aguirre," he said. "I'm here to ask you some questions about a murder investigation."

Eric kept his eyes on Ruth. "What's the matter, lady? How about a smile for me?"

Ruth tilted her head to the side and stared at Eric. "Can't," she said dryly. "My face is broken."

Eric stared at her for a second, then threw his head back and laughed.

"All right," he said, swiping at the corners of his eyes. "I like you." He nodded, then looked at Julian. "Detective, huh?"

Julian bit the inside of his cheek to hide a grin. Next to him, he felt Ruth relax. It seemed he'd underestimated her.

"That's correct," he said. "I'm here to talk to you about a murder investigation."

Eric's dark eyes narrowed. "I need my lawyer?"

Julian shrugged. "If you want. I'm just here for information."

"Huh." Eric considered him for a moment, then nodded. "All right. What do you want to know?"

"Are you a member of the Rising Suns gang?"

"You know I am." Eric pulled down the V-neck of his shirt, revealing the details of the sun tattoo at the base of his neck. He winked at Ruth, then released the fabric.

"What can you tell me about the murders of Gregory and Isabella Pushkin?"

Eric's face went blank. He pretended to think, then shook his head. "The names aren't familiar."

"You're lying." Ruth's voice was quiet in the room, but both men turned to look at her. "You do know them."

Eric shifted in his seat. "What are you, psychic or something?"

"No," she said. "But I'm not an idiot."

"They were killed six years ago, in a home invasion in Copper Cove," Julian said. "The case was all over the news."

Eric nodded. "Okay. Yeah, I think I know what you're talking about."

"There's some new evidence in the case that suggests the gang was responsible for their murders." Julian had to tread carefully here. If he revealed too much, it would put Sam in danger and it might make the gang act on their threats to Lily and Ruth. Even though Eric was in prison, Julian knew he was still in contact with members on the outside.

"How about that," Eric said flatly. "Still doesn't explain why you're here, though. I'm not the only gang member in prison."

"That's true," Julian admitted. "But the thing is, some of this new evidence suggests you were at the Pushkin house that night."

Eric smiled, but it didn't reach his eyes. "I'm afraid you're mistaken," he said. "I already told you, I don't know them."

Julian leaned forward, sensing his window of opportunity was closing. "Let's cut the crap. I don't want you. You're already in prison, serving a life sentence."

"So why are you here?"

"I want to know who sent you. Who put that target on the Pushkins' backs and sent you after them?"

Eric considered him for a moment, the wheels in his head turning. Julian held his breath, hoping this gambit would work…

"What's in it for me?" he asked finally. "Like you said, I'm already in prison. Why should I help you?"

Satisfaction rose in Julian's chest, but he kept his expression neutral. "You know life could always get better. Or worse," he added.

"Enlighten me," Eric said.

Julian shrugged, as though he didn't care either way. "Arizona is hot. Wouldn't you like to go someplace nice? Where you could go outside and not risk heatstroke?"

"What else?"

"I'm sure you know there are certain perks to helping out. Better job assignments, commissary credits."

Eric snorted. "You think I'm gonna turn into a rat for some cigarettes? Do better, man."

"Fine." Julian narrowed his eyes. "You have a parole hearing coming up in a few months. Having a cop speak on your behalf would carry a lot of weight."

Eric nodded. "That's more like it." He leaned forward. "I want a transfer. And you'd better show up at my parole hearing."

"Only if you give me a name."

Eric leaned back. "Tell you what. You come back here with my transfer papers in hand, and I'll tell you everything you want to know."

Julian ground his back teeth together. He was so close to getting the information he needed! "You gotta give me something first," he said. "I'm not going to help you unless I know you can deliver what I need."

Eric tilted his head to the side. "All right. I can respect that. So here you go. This one came from the top."

"The top?" Julian repeated. "As in, someone in a position of power ordered you to kill them?"

Eric held his hands up. "Hey, I never said I did anything."

"Yeah, yeah." Julian waved away his protestations of innocence. "But you know it was someone important who gave the order. How did they know the Pushkins?"

Eric shrugged. "Above my pay grade. But you know what they say. Lie down with dogs, get up with fleas."

"Who was the primary target?" Julian pressed. "Gregory or Isabella?"

"Nuh-uh," Eric said. "That's all you get. You come back with my transfer papers and we'll talk some more."

Realizing he wasn't going to get any more information out of Eric, Julian nodded. "Fine. Guard!"

Eric winked at Ruth as the guard came in and began to unfasten his cuffs from the bolt in the table. "You can come back and see me anytime, beautiful."

She shook her head as he was led out of the room. "Pass," she muttered under her breath. She gave Julian a questioning look as he stood, but he shook his head. "We'll talk in the truck," he said quietly. Everything in prison was subject to surveillance, and he didn't want anyone to hear their conversation.

He waited until they were on the road again before turning to her. "You made quite the impression," he said dryly.

"Sorry," she said. "I just wanted him to shut up, so I said the first thing that popped into my head."

Julian laughed. "It worked. You got him to start talking."

"He was definitely there that night," she said. "Did you see the way he froze when he heard the name Pushkin?"

Julian nodded. "Yes. He tried to cover it, but I knew he was lying."

"Was anything he told you helpful at all?"

"Some," Julian said. "If he's telling the truth, it sounds like someone with power and money wanted the Pushkins gone."

"Now you just have to figure out who," she said. "That won't be easy."

"It doesn't narrow the field too much," Julian said. "He was a prestigious contract attorney, and she was a prominent socialite. Their entire social circle consisted of wealthy, powerful people."

"Are you really going to get him transferred to another prison?" Ruth asked. "Or were you just telling him that to get him to talk to you?"

"I'm going to try," Julian replied. "I can't promise anything, but I can at least give it a shot."

He felt her eyes on him and glanced over to see her watching him, a strange expression on her face. "What?" he asked.

"You really don't lie, do you?"

He shook his head. "Not if I can help it."

She smiled, and he got the impression he'd just passed some kind of test. "That's good to know. So, what's our next step?"

He looked back at the road, his mind turning over this new information. It wasn't much to go on, but he'd worked with less before. "I'm not sure yet." The uncertainty was annoying, but there was one thing that made him feel better.

She'd said "our."

Friday morning

"Uh-huh. I see. Well, please tell him I called." Julian hung up the phone. "Again," he said sarcastically.

Ruth shot him a sympathetic glance. "Still brushing you off?"

He nodded. "Yeah. Every time I call, it's the same thing—the mayor is in a meeting. But when I try to set up an appointment, they tell me to call again later." He leaned back against the couch cushion and put his hands behind his head. "I'm starting to think he's avoiding me."

Ruth ran her eyes over the long lines of Julian's body, momentarily distracted by the sight of him stretched out so close to her. They'd spent the past two days working together, poring through the list of clients Gregory Pushkin's law firm had eventually sent over. It was just a list of names, with no accompanying information. Ruth thought it was a petty move, but Julian had pointed out they had technically complied with his request.

They'd started out working at the police station, but Julian had quickly decided to relocate. Sam's warning about an informant made them both worry that their actions were being scrutinized, so Julian had suggested they meet at his apartment to continue their research.

Which was how Ruth found herself sitting in a recliner with a tablet in her lap, watching as Julian put his feet up on the coffee table.

"Have you found anything?" His question cut through her thoughts, bringing her back to reality.

She shook her head slightly, casting aside her distractions. "Um, not especially. The Forsyth case was settled out of court. I don't think Gregory did much work on it—it looks like he was assigned to the case shortly before his murder, so I don't think he had time to make any enemies there."

"I think you're right." Julian dropped his arms and sat up. "So far, it looks like our most promising lead is this construction company deal."

"The one that was contracted to build the new civic center?"

Julian nodded. "Yeah. As best I can tell, Gregory's

firm was hired to draw up the contract between the city and the company for the project."

Ruth frowned. "Doesn't Copper Cove have a city attorney who does that kind of thing?"

"That's what I thought, too, but when I called their office, they told me that at that time, they didn't have the expertise in place, so they brought the law firm on to consult."

"Makes sense," Ruth said. "I consult with people all the time regarding my patients."

"I agree," Julian said. "But I'd still like to learn more about that project. However, the city's attorneys won't talk to me without permission from the mayor's office."

"And he's not taking your calls," she finished.

He gave her a lopsided smile. "Exactly."

"Well, we still have several names on the list. Maybe one of them will pan out?"

"I hope so." He stood up and stretched. Ruth forced herself to look away. She was here to help him, not ogle him!

"I'm going to grab a glass of water. Can I get you some?"

"That would be great." She watched him walk out of the room, a part of her still in disbelief that she was here, in his apartment, working with him. Even though they were focused on the case, being in Julian's home felt very personal. Almost like she was getting a peek at the man behind the curtain.

Her phone pinged and she reached for it. She groaned internally when she saw it was an email from work. That was one dilemma she hadn't solved yet. She and Julian had been trying to brainstorm ways to keep her and her patients safe from the gang when she returned to work on Monday, but short of having an officer shadow her all day, they hadn't come up with any ideas.

She pulled up the email and scanned the message. It was a reminder about the hospital fundraising gala tomorrow night. Her boss wanted to know if she was still going to attend.

Ruth's first instinct was to say no. With everything going on right now, the last thing she wanted to do was get dressed up and hobnob with a bunch of rich strangers while having to pretend like everything was fine. Ordinarily, she didn't mind attending these events, as it gave her a chance to talk about her work and how much it helped people. The hospital in general, and her department in particular, could always use more funds. But right now? She was so worried about Lily and wrapped up in this investigation that she'd make terrible company.

She clicked the button to reply, but as she began typing her message, a thought occurred to her. This was the hospital's major fundraising event of the year. If history was any indication, it would bring in a lot of wealthy potential donors. Exactly the kind of people the Pushkins had associated with. She closed her eyes, trying to remember the flyer that listed the special guests scheduled to make an appearance. If she wasn't mistaken, the mayor was on that list.

Julian walked into the room and held out a glass of water. Her growing excitement must have shown on her face, because he tilted his head to the side. "What's up?"

Ruth took the glass and smiled. "I know how you're going to talk to the mayor."

"Oh yeah?" He walked back over to the couch and sat down. "You've got a connection?"

"Something like that." She held up her phone, even though she knew he couldn't see the screen. "The hospital has a big fundraising gala tomorrow night. He's going to be there. And you're going to be my date."

Chapter Ten

Julian pulled to a stop at the curb in front of Ruth's house. He glanced in the rearview mirror for a final check of his hair and smoothed a wayward strand back into place. Then he scoffed and shook his head. Since when was he the guy who cared what his hair looked like?

But he already knew the answer. Since he was taking Ruth to the gala. He felt as nervous as a teen before prom, a sensation he hadn't experienced in years. Normally, he was in control of a situation. Tonight, though? He wasn't sure what to expect.

It wasn't just because he was going to ambush the mayor, conversationally speaking. He was rather looking forward to that part, actually. But he was keenly aware that while he was attending the gala on unofficial police business, this was a work function for Ruth. He didn't want to do anything that might jeopardize her position or make her job harder.

He climbed out of his truck and smoothed a hand down the front of his shirt. His fingers fiddled with the bow tie at his neck, and he forced himself to stop. Messing with it wasn't going to keep it straight.

His shoes clipped against the concrete as he walked up the path to her door. In some ways, it was kind of nice to get dressed up. The last time he'd worn a suit had been to a friend's wedding, and he could count on one hand the number of times he'd had to sport a tuxedo. Anticipation thrummed through his system as he rang the doorbell. Ruth had told him tonight's dress code was black-tie. What would she be wearing?

She opened the door and Julian's tongue stuck to the roof of his mouth. He simply stared at her, unable to form words.

Her dress was blue, the color of a sapphire. The fabric hugged her, and a thin silver band formed a belt just above her waist. The skirt draped to her toes, the fabric looking light and airy. She wore her hair down, the auburn strands forming loose waves around her face.

She was taller than usual, thanks to the heels she wore, and Julian liked the fact that her face was almost level with his. It would make it that much easier to lean in and kiss her...

"Hi." Her smile was warm as she looked at him. "You look great."

"So do you." He cleared his throat, unable to take his eyes off her. "You're gorgeous."

She blushed, the pink spots on her cheeks only adding to her appeal. "You clean up pretty well yourself. Come in for a minute. I left my bag on the table."

He followed her inside. The fabric of her skirt swirled and flowed as she moved, making it look as if she were floating across the floor. She was absolutely stunning, and unless he regained control, he was going to make a fool of himself and forget the point of this event.

Ruth returned a moment later, a small bag in one hand and a thin shawl draped over her shoulders. "I'm ready," she said with a smile.

They walked to the truck and he held the door open for her, then stood close to help her climb inside. She put her hand on his arm to steady herself, and he caught a whiff of her scent as she moved. She even smelled amazing, some light, floral note that made him think of summer.

Julian shut the door and walked to the driver's side, tugging on his bow tie. "Get it together," he muttered to himself. He had to stop letting his hormones run the show. He was a professional, for crying out loud! He'd faced down armed robbers, arrested murderers and testified in court without breaking a sweat. He could handle escorting a beautiful woman to a hospital fundraiser for a few hours.

He forced himself to focus on the road as he drove. If he glanced at her, he wouldn't be able to concentrate. The last thing they needed was for him to get into an accident tonight.

"I'm glad you had a tux," Ruth said.

"I don't, actually," he replied. "But I caught a break at the rental place. The pants are a little long, but they cuffed the hem for me."

"I didn't notice." Her voice sounded a little husky, and it made his skin tingle.

The drive to the venue was quick. Julian sized up the situation as he approached the restaurant. "I can't do the valet parking," he said. "I have a weapon in the truck. Want me to drop you off at the door?"

"No," she said. "I don't mind walking with you."

"Yes, ma'am," he murmured. He was glad to hear it, as he didn't like the thought of leaving her to stand by herself in front of the building. Even though the last few days had been quiet, he knew it was just a matter of time until the gang made their move. Ruth had agreed to let him station an officer at her home at night, but during the day, he kept watch over her.

He found a parking lot about half a block down the street and maneuvered into a spot. He hopped out of the truck and slid his tuxedo jacket on, then jogged around to help Ruth climb out. She pivoted in the seat, then reached out and straightened his bow tie. Her fingers grazed the skin of his neck and a shiver went down his spine. "There," she said with a smile. "Now you're ready."

Without thinking, Julian slipped his hands to Ruth's waist and lifted her out of the truck. She let out a little gasp and grabbed his shoulders as he drew her forward. The fabric of her dress was smooth against his palms, her skin warm underneath. She held his gaze as he slowly lowered her to the ground.

They stood there for a moment, his hands on her hips, hers sliding down a bit to his biceps. Her lips opened a bit, her breath coming in soft puffs that warmed the air between them.

Julian lowered his head. She lifted her chin. He'd just brushed his lips against hers when the rev of an engine cut through the air. Julian acted on instinct, stepping in front of Ruth as he pivoted toward the street. A car sped down the road, tires squealing against the asphalt. It was the same El Camino he'd seen at the diner last weekend.

No way was that a coincidence. He frowned as he turned back to Ruth. "Let's go," he said, offering her his arm. The sooner they got inside, the better. They were too exposed out here, something he'd momentarily forgotten.

She slipped her hand into the crook of his elbow. "Is everything okay?"

For a second, he considered not telling her about the car. But she was just as involved as he was at this point, and she had a right to know. "Remember last weekend, when I saw that El Camino outside the café? I thought I had seen it outside the restaurant the night before?"

She nodded. "Yes. You didn't think there were too many cars like that around here."

"Well, it's back. It just took off down the street."

"Oh." She cast a worried glance down the road, but there was nothing to see at this point. "Do you think it's someone from the gang watching us?"

"Most likely," he said. Her fingers tensed against his arm, and he slipped his other hand over hers. "It's okay. This thing is invitation only. And with such an A-list collection of guests, I'm sure there will be security on-site, as well."

"I'm not worried about the event," Ruth said as they crossed the street. "I'm worried about what happens after."

"Nothing is going to happen," Julian declared. "I told you I'd keep you safe. I meant it."

She looked up at him, trust shining in her eyes. "I

believe you," she said. "But in the end, it might not be up to you."

That's what scares me, he thought. But rather than vocalize his fears, he led her to the door of the restaurant and held it open for her.

Ruth pulled up the invitation on her phone and showed the screen to the waiting attendant. The man nodded and gestured for them to follow. He led them through the dining area, where each table sported white tablecloths and formal place settings. At the back of the restaurant was a large, open reception room. "Please, help yourself to beverages and hors d'oeuvres."

They slipped inside the room, which was already buzzing with people. A bar was set up against the far wall, and a few cocktail tables were scattered throughout. At one end of the room was a small stage occupied by a string quartet, the musicians filling the air with pleasant music. Waiters in white jackets and tails circulated through the crowd, offering canapés from silver platters. It reminded Julian of a wedding reception, but on a much grander scale.

"Can I get you something to drink?"

Ruth glanced at the bar. "Club soda and cranberry juice, please," she said. "I don't think I can handle anything stronger right now."

"Agreed," he said. Besides, he wasn't about to drink while he was working a case. "I'll be right back."

There was a short line at the bar, but it moved quickly. Julian headed back to Ruth, drinks in hand. But she wasn't alone.

"Julian, this is Dr. Fletcher. He's chair of the psychiatry department at the hospital."

He passed Ruth her drink and offered his hand. "Nice to meet you. I'm Julian Aguirre."

"Pleasure." He noted the older man's firm grip as they shook. "How do you know Ruth?"

"I'm a detective, and she helped me with one of my cases," Julian replied. It was the story they'd agreed on to explain their relationship. Truthful, but not too forthcoming.

Dr. Fletcher's eyes brightened with interest. "Oh, how wonderful." He looked at Ruth. "You must tell me more soon. I've been wondering if we can perhaps form a working group with our local law enforcement to assist them on mental distress calls. Since you already have experience working with the police, I'd love to bend your ear."

Ruth smiled. "I'd like that, sir. I'll be back in my office on Monday. Maybe we can chat sometime next week?"

"Perfect!" He beamed at her, clearly excited by the prospect. "I have to run now—my wife is waving me over." He touched her arm, then turned to Julian. "Nice to meet you."

"Likewise," Julian replied. The older man walked away, headed in the direction of a frowning woman standing by a cocktail table. "He seems nice," he remarked.

"He is," Ruth agreed. "He's always been kind to me, and he seems to have a real interest in music therapy."

"So how does this work?" Julian asked. He took a sip of his drink as he looked around the room. "It's my first time at a fundraiser. What are we supposed to do?"

"Right now, we mingle," Ruth replied. "The donors

aren't here yet. Once they arrive, the cocktails will really ramp up until dinner. There will be some remarks during the meal, and then it'll be back in here for more drinking and some dancing."

"I see." It sounded like the hospital administrators were counting on the liberal flow of alcohol to loosen the purse strings of their would-be donors. It was a classic approach, and for good reason: it usually worked.

"Are the donors always fashionably late?"

She nodded and took a sip of her drink. "Generally speaking, yes. But they should arrive anytime now, and then we'll get down to business."

"What time do you think the mayor will get here?" Julian hoped it was soon. As much as he enjoyed the sight of Ruth in her dress, he could tell by the appraising looks from some of the other men in the room that he wasn't the only one. He wanted to drape his tuxedo jacket over her shoulders to shield her from view, but realized he was being irrational. They could look all they wanted; he was the one who'd come with her, and he'd be the one to escort her home.

"Your guess is as good as mine," she said. "But I'm sure he'll be here for the meal. I've never known him to miss a chance to speak in front of a crowd."

He chuckled, knowing she was right. "Good point."

She slipped her hand into his. "Ready to meet some people?"

He squeezed her fingers. "Lead the way."

Ruth was ready to go home.

They'd been at the gala for three hours already, and her feet ached from her heels. Sitting down for dinner had helped, but now they were back in the reception room for dessert cocktails and dancing, and she'd had just about enough.

She glanced at Julian, who looked handsome as ever in his tuxedo. He'd been charming tonight, schmoozing with her colleagues and even a few donors, the very picture of a supportive boyfriend. But she could tell by the way his eyes scanned the crowd that he was anxious for the mayor to arrive.

"Maybe he's not coming."

Julian leaned down, putting his ear closer to her face. "What? I didn't hear you over the music."

The string quartet had been replaced by a three-piece band, and they were in full swing, playing a selection of hits from different eras. The dance floor was growing more crowded by the minute as couples jostled for position on the wood floor.

Ruth rose onto her toes, ignoring the protests of her feet. Her lips accidentally brushed his earlobe. "Maybe he's not coming," she said again.

Julian placed a hand on her waist to steady her, his touch warm through the thin, silky fabric of her dress. "I'm starting to think you might be right." His breath was hot against her ear and it triggered a wave of goose bumps down her arms. Suddenly, her feet didn't bother her so much anymore.

"When do you want to leave?" he asked.

Ruth shrugged. At this point, she'd done her duty. She didn't have to stay any longer. But she didn't want to miss the mayor's arrival.

If he was even coming.

"We can go whenever," she said.

Julian nodded. "Will you give me another fifteen minutes? If he hasn't shown up by then, he's not going to."

"That's fine." She could do that. Her feet could handle a quarter of an hour, no problem.

The corner of Julian's mouth lifted in a mischievous grin. "Wanna dance to pass the time?"

Ruth's first instinct was to refuse. Her feet were back to hurting, and she was self-conscious at the thought of dancing. But Julian's expression was so hopeful she couldn't bear to disappoint him.

"All right," she said. "But I'm not very good."

"You'll be fine," he said. "I can show you some moves."

He took her hand and led her to the dance floor. They found a spot in the corner, and for the next few minutes, he taught her a simple box step in time with the beat. Soon, Ruth was laughing, the pain in her feet forgotten.

The band wrapped up the fast song and launched into a slow one. Julian didn't miss a step. He reached for her, drawing her close to him. He cradled her right hand by his shoulder, his arm forming a solid band at her lower back.

Ruth's breath caught in her throat as their bodies brushed. Her skin tingled, feeling suddenly too tight. Julian smiled down at her, his face striking in the strobe lights from the stage.

He was so close. Close enough to finish that kiss they'd started in the parking lot. His fingers splayed against her back as he guided her around their little corner of the dance floor with gentle nudges.

Ruth felt like she was floating in his arms. She'd

never thought of herself as graceful, but Julian was an amazing partner. She found herself anticipating his next move, their bodies syncing as they swayed to the music.

All too soon, the song was over. But even as the last notes faded into the air, Julian still held her close. "Where did you learn to dance?" she asked.

"I took lessons for a friend's wedding," he said. "All the other groomsmen hated it, but I thought it was fun."

There was a stir at the front of the room, and they looked over to see the mayor, grinning and shaking hands as he walked into the crowd.

"About time," Julian muttered. He led Ruth off the dance floor, on a mission to intercept the mayor. But it seemed the mayor had plans of his own. He made his way to the stage and grabbed the microphone.

"Folks, I'm sorry I'm so late getting here. I'm coming from another event that just wrapped up. I want to take a minute to thank you all for your generosity toward our amazing hospital. I was informed on my way up here that you all raised over one million dollars tonight!"

A cheer rose from the crowd and people started clapping. The mayor smiled and nodded, waiting for the applause to die down. "I know our hospital is going to put that money to good use, helping the people of this great city!"

More applause. Ruth looked over to find Julian watching the show, his expression skeptical. He leaned over to her. "He's acting like he's running for election in a huge metropolis."

Ruth nodded. The man definitely had the politician act down pat.

After a few more remarks, the mayor left the stage.

Julian grabbed her hand and positioned them at the edge of the circle of people that had formed around the man. As soon as there was a lull in the conversation, Julian jumped in.

"Mr. Mayor, I'm Detective Julian Aguirre."

"Nice to meet you, Detective. I always enjoy speaking to a member of our fine police force."

Julian grinned. To everyone else, the expression probably looked friendly. But Ruth saw the intensity in his eyes and knew his smile was more of a warning.

"I'm glad to hear that, sir. You see, I've been in contact with your office several times over the past few days, trying to set up an appointment with you."

"Oh? How can I help?"

"I'm working on a murder investigation, and I need to ask you a few questions."

At the words "murder investigation," a hush fell over the gathered crowd.

The mayor glanced around and laughed nervously. "Murder? I don't know how I can assist you with that."

"It's a cold case," Julian explained. "Maybe you remember the Pushkin murders from six years ago?"

The mayor's smile faltered. "Of course. Terrible tragedy." He tried to move, but Julian stepped in his way, blocking his path.

"I agree. So I'm sure you won't mind if I stop by your office Monday morning to talk to you?"

"Of course not. I'm always happy to help an officer." The man was visibly uncomfortable, but with so many eyes on him, he was trapped.

Julian smiled again. "Wonderful. I'll see you at eight sharp." He stepped back to let the man pass, and most of the crowd followed. A few people remained behind, whispering to one another.

Ruth reached for his hand. "I think it's time to leave."

"Lead the way." He tucked her hand into the crook of his arm and together they stepped outside.

Ruth shivered as the chilly air hit her bare skin. "Wait," Julian instructed. He released her hand and shrugged off his jacket. Before she could protest, he draped it around her shoulders, then took her hand again.

"Thanks," she said, snuggling into the warm fabric. It even smelled like him, a combination of coffee and a woodsy note that likely came from his soap. She felt surrounded by him, her senses filled with different aspects of Julian.

"I think that went well," he said as they walked to the parking lot. "I mean, it's clear the mayor isn't happy about our appointment, but I'm satisfied."

"I'm glad you got to talk to him," Ruth said. "I'd have felt bad if we'd gotten all dressed up for nothing."

They stopped at his truck, and Julian stared down at her, his eyes as dark as the night sky above. "I wouldn't say it was for nothing." He ran a fingertip along the edge of his jacket lapel, touching the bare skin of her neck underneath.

Ruth shivered, but it had nothing to do with the cold and everything to do with the man standing in front of her.

Julian dipped his head and her heart nearly skipped a beat. *Yes! It's finally happening!*

He kissed her, his mouth fitting over hers with a gentle pressure that sent zings of sensation through her body. His lips were surprisingly soft and so warm. He pulled her closer.

She wasn't sure how long it lasted. Julian leaned back and smiled down at her. "I've been wanting to do that all night," he admitted, his voice husky.

"What a coincidence," Ruth said. "I've been wanting you to do that all night." It was true; ever since she'd opened her door and seen the look on his face, she'd hoped they might share a kiss. And now that they had, she couldn't wait to do it again.

"All you have to do is—" Julian stopped talking, a strange expression stealing over his face as he cocked his head, listening to something.

Ruth heard it a second later—the roar of a car engine. Then she heard a strange metallic click.

"Get down!" Julian shoved her roughly to the ground. The back of her head hit the pavement with a *thunk*, and she cried out. But before she could ask what was happening, Julian threw himself on top of her, nearly crushing her chest with his weight.

Everything seemed to happen in slow motion. She watched from under his truck as a set of wheels rolled by, slowing as they passed the parking lot. Then she heard a series of loud pops that sounded like cannons going off. Julian's truck shook above her, glass shattering and falling to the ground. Ruth screamed and turned her face to the side as the shards rained down. Julian crawled up her body, shielding her head with his chest.

In a matter of seconds, it was over. Tires squealed as the car sped away, leaving them alone.

Julian didn't move right away. Ruth started to panic, fearing the worst.

"Julian!" She tried to lift her hands, but they were trapped at her sides by his weight. "Talk to me!" she pleaded. *Please, let him be okay*, she prayed silently. She couldn't lose him now, not when they were starting to open up to each other!

He moved slowly, raising himself off her by degrees. He angled down so he could see her. "Are you okay?" he asked. One of his hands touched the side of her face, tracing her cheekbone. "Were you hit?"

Ruth shook her head, wincing as the movement sent a spike of pain through her skull. "I don't think so. But I've got a bump on my head. Are you okay?"

Julian moved to crouch beside her, helping her sit up. "I'm good. They missed."

"Thank God," she said. The shock of the event was wearing off, and she started to tremble.

"Someone is definitely looking out for us tonight," Julian said. He put his arm around her and drew her close. "Come on. We can't stay in the open right now."

"Where are we going?" She glanced at his truck. She couldn't see the side that had been facing the road, but all the windows were broken. It definitely wasn't going anywhere soon.

"Back to the party," Julian said shortly. "We'll wait for the police there."

Ruth clung to him as they made their way back down the street. Her body ached, but at least she was still alive.

"Julian?" Even her voice was starting to shake.

"Yeah?" He kept looking ahead, scanning the area for more threats as he led her to the relative safety of the restaurant and the crowd within.

"Thank you."

His lips pressed together in a thin line. "Don't thank me. I'm the one who got you into this."

"You saved my life."

He glanced at her then, his face softening a bit. "Always."

Chapter Eleven

"We're almost done. Just a few more minutes, okay?"

Ruth looked up at him and nodded, though he could tell she was exhausted. The blue and red lights strobed across her face but did nothing to mask her fatigue.

It had been an hour since the drive-by shooting. Thankfully, his brothers in arms had responded quickly to the call. Forensics was examining his truck now, a veritable campsite of evidence markers spread around his vehicle, each one indicating the location of a bullet casing.

The ambulance had come and gone. Ruth had insisted she was fine, but Julian had put his foot down and bullied her into letting the paramedics examine her. Only after they'd declared she was uninjured did he start to relax and take full breaths again.

This should never have happened. He should have listened to his instincts and gotten her out of there when the car had driven past the first time. He'd been so intent on talking to the mayor that he'd brushed off the warning sign, choosing to believe it was surveillance rather than a foreshadowing of what was to come.

Thank God he'd heard the engine before they started shooting. Thank God he'd shoved her to the ground, knocking her out of the path of the bullets. And thank God the shooter hadn't had better aim.

"I owe You one," he muttered to himself.

After wrapping up his statement, he flagged down a uniformed officer. "Can you give us a ride?"

"Sure," the young man said. "Where to?"

"Plaza Hotel," Julian replied.

Ruth spoke up. "What? No, I want to go home."

Julian shook his head. "Not tonight. Sorry."

"Please?" She looked so fragile, standing there in his tuxedo jacket, her hair a mess and her makeup smudged. He hated to disappoint her, but she'd been in enough danger tonight.

"You can't," he said, trying to be gentle. "The gang just tried to kill us. Where do you think they're going to go when they realize we're not dead?"

Understanding dawned on her face. "Oh," she said dully. She didn't protest as Julian led her to the squad car and helped her into the back seat. He slid in next to her and put his arm around her.

At least she wasn't trembling anymore. It was a good sign.

They were silent on the short drive to the hotel. The officer pulled into the circular drive, then hopped out and opened the back door. "Is there anything else I can do for you, sir?" he asked eagerly.

"Not tonight. Thanks for your help." He glanced at

the young man's nameplate and committed it to memory. "Be safe out there."

"You, too," the man said.

Julian led Ruth into the hotel and lingered by the entrance as he watched the officer drive away. Once he was certain the car was gone, he tugged Ruth outside again.

"What's going on?" she asked as they crossed the street.

"Just being careful," he said as they walked into the lobby of the Fairmont Resort.

She glanced back to the street. "You think he's the one feeding information to the gang?" she whispered.

Julian shrugged. "I have no idea," he said, keeping his voice low. "But right now, I don't trust anybody."

They approached the desk clerk, whose professional smile stayed firmly in place as he took in their appearances. "We need two rooms," Julian said. "Adjacent, please."

"Very good," the man said. "Just for the night?"

Julian nodded. The clerk typed on his keyboard for a few seconds, then glanced up. "I have a set on the fifth floor. Will that work?"

"Great," Julian replied. He slid his credit card and driver's license across the counter and waited for the man to complete the reservations. "Do you guys have a gift shop?"

The clerk's eyes flicked to Ruth. "We do. Just around the corner, and to your left. It's closing in twenty minutes."

"Good to know. Thanks." He accepted his cards back, then took the keycards to their rooms.

The clerk used the tip of his pen to point to their room numbers. "Use the elevators around the corner. They're across from the gift shop. Enjoy your stay."

Buddy, if you only knew, Julian thought as they stepped away from the counter.

"Come on," he said to Ruth. "We need some new clothes."

They ducked into the gift shop and emerged fifteen minutes later with all the basics. Shortly after, he used the keycard to unlock one of their rooms.

"This one will be yours," he said. He walked over to the door that connected their rooms and unlocked it from her side. "Stay put," he instructed, as he walked back into the hall.

His room was a mirror image of hers. After snapping the dead bolt into place, he opened his side of the connecting doors and walked back into Ruth's room. She hadn't moved from her spot by the television. She was standing still, staring into space but not really looking at anything.

Julian made sure the door to the hallway was locked, and jammed the small recliner under the handle for good measure. He didn't think the gang would find them tonight, but he wasn't going to take any chances.

"Ruth?" She didn't respond, so he carefully reached out and touched her shoulder. She let out a strangled shriek and jumped at the contact.

"I'm sorry," he said, holding his hands up. "I didn't mean to scare you."

She shook her head, visibly clearing her thoughts. "It's okay. I just got lost there for a minute."

"Understandable." Tonight had been stressful, to

say the least. He'd been shot at a few times before in his career, but never like that. It was an experience he wouldn't soon forget, and he could only imagine what it was like from Ruth's perspective.

"The good news is, you're safe tonight. You can rest now."

She blinked back tears as she looked up at him. "Do you really think so?"

He nodded. "Yes. I'll be on the other side of that door. If you need anything, just call out." He started to walk toward the door, desperate for a shower.

"Julian?"

Her voice stopped him and he turned. "Yes?"

She stood there, chewing on her thumbnail. Her dress was stained from the oil on the asphalt of the parking lot, and the broken glass had ripped the delicate fabric in several places. But she was still so beautiful, even in the tatters. "Can we leave the doors open?"

"Of course."

Before he knew what she was doing, she closed the distance between them and threw herself against him. He wrapped his arms around her, holding her close.

She gripped him tightly, her fingers digging into his back. Julian dipped his head, his nose pressing into her hair. He inhaled deeply, drawing her scent into his lungs.

Too close. He'd come too close to losing her tonight. It was a wonder she hadn't been hurt. He sent up another prayer of thanksgiving, grateful that God had helped him protect her.

"It's going to be okay," he said softly, stroking his hand down her back.

"I know," she said, her voice muffled against his chest. "Just don't leave me."

"I won't." It was more than a statement; it was a promise. He wasn't going to walk away from her, especially not while the gang was still after them. He'd do just about anything to keep her safe.

She sighed in his arms, some of the tension leaving her body. With a final squeeze, she released him and stepped back. "Oh no," she said, sounding dismayed. "I got makeup on your white shirt."

He glanced down and shrugged. "No worries. Not like I was going to get the deposit back on this tux anyway."

There was a beat of silence, and then Ruth started to laugh. Julian grinned at the sound, his heart lightening. They'd made it through tonight. They'd figure out what to do tomorrow.

For now, they had each other.

Ruth woke slowly, her muscles protesting as she stretched. Why did the back of her head hurt? And why did she feel like she'd been run over by a truck?

She opened her eyes, registering the unfamiliar room. The events of last night came rushing back.

The gala. The shooting.

Julian saving her life.

She sat up, searching for him. Was he okay? He'd seemed fine last night, but maybe something had happened...

The soft sounds of light snores drifted into her room from the open doors that connected their suites. True to his word, he'd left the adjoining doors open last night so she didn't feel so alone. It seemed like he was always looking out for her.

She slipped out of bed and gently shut her side of the doors. Just because she was awake didn't mean Julian had to be. After a quick stop in the bathroom, she started to make coffee.

She'd just taken the first sip when there was a soft knock. "Come in," she called.

Julian slowly pushed open the door, peering into her room. "I smelled coffee. Is there more where that came from?"

"Of course." She brewed him a cup and took a seat on one end of the sofa, leaving room for him on the other side. He sank down to the cushions and took a sip, then groaned.

"Just what I needed," he breathed.

She smiled, but it didn't last long. The worries and stress from last night were returning full force, their weight settling over her shoulders like a yoke. Surviving a drive-by shooting had left Ruth feeling closer to Julian than ever. But she had to be careful—she couldn't let the emotions of their brush with death cloud her judgment or cause their relationship to move too fast.

But they weren't the only ones in the gang's line of fire.

"Is Lily still okay?"

Julian looked at her over the rim of his mug. "I haven't checked in with the officers at her home yet, but I'm assuming so. They would have called me if anything had happened last night."

Ruth nodded, some of her fears easing. In the aftermath of last night's shooting, Julian had ordered an additional car to guard Lily's family. But thankfully, it seemed they had been the only targets.

"What happens now?"

He frowned. "I go to work."

Of course. Because ultimately, a drive-by attempted murder wasn't the worst thing he'd dealt with in his career. It was just another reminder of how different their worlds were compared to each other. When she had a bad day, everyone still went home alive and unharmed. But Julian couldn't say the same.

Ruth took a sip of her coffee, considering the day ahead. "You know, I haven't missed church on Sunday in a long time."

Julian's expression was sympathetic. "I'm sorry, Ruth."

She shrugged. "It's fine. I'm sure God will understand."

"Will you tell me about your church?"

He seemed genuinely interested, which surprised her a little. But he'd told her earlier he'd started praying again. Maybe he was strengthening his faith?

"I think you'd really like it," she said. "The people are friendly and welcoming, and Pastor Nichols always makes me think with his sermons."

Julian smiled. "You sing in the choir, don't you? I'd like to see that."

"You should come to a service." She reached out and grabbed his hand, excited by the thought of having him there. Her church family was an important part of her life, one she'd love to share with Julian.

"I will." He was quiet a moment. "I've been praying more lately." He sounded almost shy.

Warmth bloomed in Ruth's chest. "I'm glad to hear it."

"You said something, at our first meeting. About forgiveness." His expression was serious as he looked at her. "I've been thinking about it ever since."

She laughed, flattered to know she'd had such an impact. "Really? What was it?"

"You said forgiveness isn't something you just do once. It's a choice you have to keep making, over and over again."

Ruth nodded. "Who are you forgiving?" she asked quietly.

"My dad," he said. "And…myself."

She'd expected him to say his father. But himself? What could Julian have done that he felt required forgiveness?

"Why do you need to forgive yourself?"

He met her eyes and the emotion she saw in his gaze made her heart ache. He looked like a man at war with himself, one who was desperate for relief but too scared to reach for it.

"Julian," she said softly. She set her mug on the coffee table, then reached for his and did the same. Taking both his hands in hers, she moved closer to him. "Talk to me."

He was silent for so long that she feared he wasn't going to talk. Then he opened his mouth, his voice halting as he began to speak.

"My father called me. The day he died. It was just after his indictment had been handed down. He knew he'd been caught, and that the charges weren't going to go away."

He paused, and Ruth resisted the urge to fill the silence with a question. This was Julian's story; she had to let him tell it his own way.

"We argued for a bit, back and forth. Then he stopped trying to defend himself, and he asked if I'd ever be able to forgive him."

Ruth squeezed his hands in a gesture of silent support.

"I told him no. I thought he was just trying to dodge responsibility for his actions." He shook his head. "He died by suicide a few hours later."

"I'm so sorry," Ruth whispered.

"It's my fault," Julian said. Tears shone in his eyes as he looked at her. "If I'd just said yes, or even told him I'd think about it, he might not have done it."

"You don't know that," Ruth replied. "You were being honest, and you were in pain. You weren't trying to be deliberately cruel."

"But the outcome was the same. I might not have meant to break his heart, but that's what happened."

She could see she wasn't getting through to him, so she tried a different approach. "What does your family think?"

He looked down. "I never told them."

"Oh, Julian," she whispered. No wonder he seemed so tortured. He'd convinced himself he was responsible for his father's suicide, then cut himself off from his family out of fear. "You need to talk to them."

"I know. I just…" He trailed off, shaking his head. "I'm not ready to lose them, too."

"How do you know you will?" she asked. "Maybe your dad called your brother before talking to you. Maybe he spoke to your mother, as well. You've spent all this time thinking he called only you, that you were the one to drive him to kill himself. But what if that's not true? What if your brother said the same thing? Your mother? They were just as affected by his actions, just as hurt."

He blinked at her, clearly considering the possibility for the first time. "I...I hadn't thought of that," he admitted.

"Even if your father didn't speak to them, his actions are his own," she said. "I think he'd made up his mind before he called you."

"Maybe he was trying to say goodbye," Julian said. He frowned. "Maybe I missed the signs because I was so angry with him."

Ruth nodded, encouraging him. "Let me ask you this—if your brother came to you and told you he'd spoken to your dad before his death, and he thought he was responsible because of what he'd said to your father, what would you do?"

"I'd tell him he was wrong, that it wasn't his fault," Julian replied automatically.

Ruth smiled. "Then give yourself that same grace."

He shook his head. "You make it sound so easy."

She laughed. "It's not easy, believe me! I spent many years thinking I was responsible for my sister's death. If I had walked a little faster, we'd have made it to the curb before that car came flying down the street. If I hadn't stopped to pet that dog, we wouldn't have been there. Or maybe if we'd stayed a little longer, the car would've passed us by. So many different scenarios. So many ways to blame myself. But I eventually realized that my mental gymnastics were keeping me rooted in the past. One of my counselors told me it was okay for me to move on. Letting go of my pain and self-blame didn't mean I was going to forget my sister. It took a long time, but I discovered that once I stopped obsessing over her death, I had room to remember and celebrate her life."

A flicker of hope shone in Julian's eyes. "That's really beautiful," he said. "I'm glad you found peace."

"You can, too," she told him. "It won't happen overnight, but you can get to a point where you remember the good times with your father, instead of focusing on his betrayal."

"I hope you're right," he said. "I would like that."

She squeezed his hands again. "When this is over, come to a Sunday service with me. It's easier to go through these things when you have support. There's a men's group at my church you might like. If they're anything like my women's group, it'll be a great support network for you."

"Okay." He nodded, determination filling his eyes. "You've talked me into it."

Ruth smiled, happy to know he was going to give it a chance. It felt so normal, to make plans for the future. But…would they even have a future?

Julian must have sensed the change in her mood. "What's wrong?" he asked.

She shook her head. "I was just wondering if we'll even be around to go to a service."

"Yes," he said firmly. "We will." He reached for their mugs, then tipped his head back and drained the last of his coffee. "Let's get dressed."

"Where are we going?" She felt a spike of alarm

at the thought of leaving the hotel. The logical part of her knew they couldn't stay here forever, but this had turned into a safe haven, a shelter from the real world. She didn't want the experience to end.

Her doubts started up again. Was this what a relationship with Julian would be like? Obviously not every case he worked would involve a murderous gang bent on silencing him, but as a police officer, he dealt with dangerous people every day. What if he was injured, or worse? Could she handle being with him, knowing that he could be taken from her at any time? Would her heart be able to handle the loss of another person close to her?

Julian spoke, interrupting her thoughts. "I'm going to the precinct. You're coming with me."

"Do you think that's safe?" she asked. "We still don't know who's feeding the gang information."

"I know," he replied. "But I've got a plan."

Chapter Twelve

The station was a hum of activity by the time Julian and Ruth arrived.

"Is it always this busy on a Sunday?" she asked.

"They tried to kill a cop last night," Julian explained. "It's all hands on deck right now."

Ruth frowned at his explanation, but she didn't say anything.

He led her to a small conference room. "Sit tight. I'll be right back."

He left her there and headed for Lieutenant Pierce's office.

The older man glanced up at Julian's knock. "Aguirre!" He got to his feet, relief etched on his face. "Glad to see you're okay."

"Thanks, sir," Julian responded. He walked in and took a chair across from the lieutenant's desk. "Any progress?"

"We found an El Camino matching your description about an hour ago. Arrested the two men inside. No guns recovered, but they're being processed for gun-shot residue as we speak."

"Excellent. Listen, I have a favor to ask." He filled Pierce in on the fact that someone on the force was feeding the gang information. "I think I know who it might be."

Pierce listened to his plan, nodding. "All right. We'll play along. We'll keep news of the arrests under wraps, for now."

"Got a mug shot I can see?"

Pierce typed on his keyboard, then flipped his monitor screen around. Julian studied the image of the man, committing it to memory.

"Okay, thanks. I'll make the call now."

He left Pierce's office and returned to the conference room. "Here's the plan," he told Ruth.

She listened, eyes growing wider as he filled her in. "What makes you so sure it's her?"

"It's the timing of it. The gang knew awfully fast Lily had been here and described a face to us. I have a hard time thinking anyone who's helped on this case would undermine the investigation like that."

Ruth lifted one eyebrow, her expression skeptical. "I know," he said, staving off her objection. "No one is perfect. You and I both have a history with police corruption. But until I can prove otherwise, I want to be able to trust the people I'm working with."

"How are you going to prove she's the one?"

"I'm going to call her in and describe a suspect from the shooting last night. I'll tell her we arrested one of the men responsible. Then I'm going to wait to see how long it takes the gang to get that information."

"I didn't know you'd seen anyone," she said, sounding surprised.

"I didn't," he said. "But what she doesn't know is

that we've already arrested both of the guys. They're being processed as we speak."

"Oh." Understanding dawned on her face. "Since that hasn't made the news yet, you'll know if she tells them."

"Exactly." He held up his phone. "I know Sam said I shouldn't contact him, but in this case, I'm going to have to make an exception."

At that moment, his phone dinged with an incoming message. He glanced at the screen and smiled. Perfect timing.

Sam's message was short and sweet. Status?

Julian typed back. Still breathing.

Sam sent him a thumbs-up. Julian replied, Know who it was?

Yes.

But you can't tell me?

Yes.

Do you have eyes on them?

There was a short delay, then Sam's reply arrived. Actually, no. Searching now.

Let me know when you find them. I have a theory.

Sam sent back a bunch of question marks. Julian laughed.

All in good time. Stay safe.

He glanced up from his phone to find Ruth watching him, a smile playing at the corners of her mouth. "Let me guess? Sam?"

Julian nodded.

"Have you talked to him at all? Since…that night?"

"No." Sam's involvement was something he was going to have to deal with, but not now.

"So what do you need me to do?"

Julian simply stared at Ruth, impressed once more by her absolute willingness to help. Despite the fact there'd been an attempt on her life last night and her world had been flipped upside down, she was calm and collected and eager to work. Most people would still be in shock or bemoaning their situation. But not her. She was remarkable.

And he wanted her in his life. Not just now, but for the long haul.

The intensity of his desire nearly stole his breath. He had the sudden, ridiculous urge to drop to his knees and beg her to stay with him. She made him better, helped him see different angles of a situation. And she'd shown him he didn't have to live under the shadow of his guilt anymore. It would take some work, but for the first time in a long time, he had hope that he might be able to move on from his father's crimes and subsequent suicide.

"Just sit with me, will you? I'd like you there when I talk to her."

"Of course." She smiled, making the room seem brighter. "I won't go anywhere."

Ruth sat next to Julian as he described the face of the man who had tried to kill them last night. She studied the sketch artist as she worked, admiring her skill and speed. It didn't take long for her to render an image. Ruth didn't know if it was a good likeness or not, as she hadn't seen the man. But Julian nodded and said it was accurate.

She watched as the woman packed up her supplies, wondering if Julian was right. Was the sketch artist the one who was in contact with the Rising Suns? It seemed far-fetched, but what did Ruth know? Julian had been a detective for many years, and she trusted his instincts.

As the woman leaned forward to collect a wayward pencil, the pendant she wore on a chain around her neck slipped free of her shirt. Ruth nearly gasped when she saw a stylized sun carved into a small silver disc. It wasn't the same image as Eric's tattoo, but talk about a coincidence.

She glanced over to see if Julian had noticed. He was looking in another direction, so she tapped his leg under the table and scratched her throat. Julian's eyes cut to the sketch artist and he went very still when he saw her necklace.

"Thanks again, Marie," he said, pushing back from the table as the woman rose.

"No problem," she said with a smile. "I'm glad you two are okay. Hopefully you'll find this guy soon."

Ruth stepped to the door with them. "I like your necklace," she said.

Marie's hand flew to the charm and she tucked it back underneath her shirt. "Thanks," she said lightly. "My boyfriend gave it to me."

Ruth smiled. "Gifts in small boxes are always nice."

Marie laughed. "I'm still hoping for a ring." She crossed her fingers and held them up by her head.

"Maybe soon?" Ruth suggested.

"I'll tell him you said that!"

"We'll see you next time, Marie," Julian said. They watched as she walked through the sprawl of desks and headed for the door of the station.

Ruth turned to look at Julian. "I hate to say it, but I hope you're wrong. She seems nice."

"I'm sure she is," Julian replied. "But I'm not wrong. Did you see how she reacted when you commented on her necklace?"

"Maybe she doesn't know what it means?" Ruth said hopefully. "Maybe she really likes summer, or has some other connection to the sun?"

Julian shook his head, smiling. "I love that you try to see the best in people. But she knows what it means. If she didn't, why was she so quick to tuck it away again?"

"I suppose," Ruth grumbled. Part of her hoped this was all just a misunderstanding. Although, if that was true, then the identity of the mole would still be a mystery. She sighed, realizing there were no easy answers here. Either the nice-seeming sketch artist was the gang's source, or one of Julian's fellow officers was involved. For his sake, she hoped that wasn't the case.

"And now we wait," he said.

As it turned out, they didn't have to wait very long. A few minutes after Marie left, Julian's phone dinged with an incoming message. He glanced at the screen, then turned it so she could read the message.

One arrested, one at large. But you already knew that.

"There we go," he said simply.

Ruth nodded, relieved at the fact that at least one problem had been solved today.

Julian stepped out to talk to another officer, presumably to ask her to arrest Marie. He stepped back inside the room, then groaned when his phone rang.

"Aguirre."

Ruth watched his face change as he listened to the person on the other end of the line. His expression morphed from neutral to disbelief to anger, all in the space of a few minutes.

Oh no. A growing sense of unease began to brew in her stomach. Something was wrong. Again.

Lily? she wondered. But no. If something had happened to the girl, Julian wouldn't be so composed.

Still, as soon as he ended the call she had to ask. "Is Lily okay?"

He glanced at her. "As far as I know. That was the DA's office. I called them earlier in the week to ask about the possibility of getting Eric transferred."

"I take it the answer is no?"

"Doesn't matter anymore," Julian said. "Eric is dead."

"What?" The news came as a surprise. "Marie didn't know about our visit to talk to him." Which meant…

Julian nodded. "The Rising Suns aren't taking any chances."

"But how did they know we were there? Who could have told them?" It didn't make any sense. They hadn't been followed by anyone, and the man was in prison. Who was he going to tell?

Julian gave her one of those looks that told her she was being naive. "Prison isn't as locked down as you think," he said. "News is currency, and a lot of guys are still part of the same gangs they belong to on the outside."

"So you think another one of the Rising Suns did this?"

Julian shrugged. "I don't know. But this puts Sam in a precarious position. If what he says is true, Eric pulled the trigger that night. He's dead now, which means the only other person who could take the fall for the Pushkin murders is him."

A chill skittered down Ruth's spine. "They're either going to kill him or throw him under the bus."

Julian's expression was grave. "And since the police won't let him be prosecuted, they'll know he's undercover."

"Which would make him an even bigger target," Ruth finished. "How can we help him?"

"By figuring out who is calling the shots," Julian said. "If I can bring down the person who paid the gang to murder the Pushkins, it'll take the heat off Sam."

Ruth shook her head, a hopeless feeling stealing over her. "Where do we even start?"

"We go back to the beginning," Julian said. "And hope we can beat the clock."

Chapter Thirteen

They worked long into the night, holed up in that conference room. Someone ordered a pizza around midnight, and the hot, cheesy food gave them a second wind.

Just as he'd said, they'd started from the beginning. This time, Julian had focused on the contract Gregory Pushkin had been working on for the city. He'd called in a few favors at the courthouse and been granted access to some of the documents without having to go through all the red tape. Ruth had been poring over those while he searched for more information on Eric. Sam had said the man had powerful friends, so why hadn't they protected him?

Through it all, Ruth had stayed by his side. He was grateful for her company on so many levels: he didn't have to worry about her going home and she was an extra pair of eyes and ears to help him examine documents and to talk through some of his wilder ideas. But more importantly, he just liked being around her. He'd gotten used to her presence over the past week. It was going to be hard when things went back to normal and she returned to her job.

"Julian? This sounds interesting."

Her voice cut through his thoughts and he shook off his fatigue to focus on her face. "Let's hear it."

Ruth frowned as she read from a sheet of paper. "According to this newspaper article, the construction company who built the conference center was not the lowest bidder."

"Okay," he said, trying to follow her train of thought.

"This article came out a few months after they broke ground. The project had stalled, and people wanted to know why. This guy did some digging and discovered the construction company was refusing to work until the city coughed up more money. They said unexpected expenses had come up, and they needed more funds."

Julian leaned forward. "So they were essentially holding the city hostage?"

She nodded. "That's what it looks like. Anyway, he reports that he tried to find out more about the company, but was stonewalled."

"Did he file any more articles?"

"Let me check." She turned to the computer and began typing. A few seconds later, she gasped. "You're not going to believe this."

"Try me," he said.

"The reporter is dead. He died a few weeks after this article was printed."

Julian's skin started to tingle. They were getting close. He could feel it.

"How did he die?" he asked carefully. He was trying

not to get his hopes up, but something told him this was exactly the lead they'd been looking for.

"Car accident." She leaned to the side and gave him a skeptical look. "Sounds a little too convenient, if you ask me."

"There are no coincidences," Julian said. Adrenaline pumped through his system, sharpening his mind. "So here's how it went down," he said, thinking out loud. "Gregory Pushkin is assigned to examine the contract between the city and this construction company. He does his due diligence and discovers something about the company he doesn't like. He starts to raise a stink about it, so they shut him up. The deal goes through. When things start to go wrong and a reporter begins asking questions, they get rid of him, too."

Ruth nodded. "Sounds plausible to me. The only problem is, who is 'they'?"

"I don't know." He leaned back in his chair, shaking his head. "It has to be someone with connections to the gang. Someone who knows they can use the gang as their own personal contract killers."

"A friend? Family member?" Ruth suggested.

Julian's mind turned over possibilities. "Maybe…" But how did it all fit together? Was Eric's powerful friend the one who'd ordered the job? And when Eric became a liability, had they been the one to order him killed?

"Julian…" Ruth's tone was uncharacteristically heavy. He glanced up to see her sporting a scandalized expression. "Do you think it could be the mayor?" She practically whispered the words, as though afraid someone might hear her.

His jaw dropped as the pieces clicked into place. A powerful friend. Someone who needed that construction deal to go through so he could win reelection. Someone who perhaps stood to gain financially from the project?

"Ruth," he breathed. "I think you might be right."

To his surprise, she leaned back in the chair, her face losing color. "Ruth?" he asked. "Are you okay?"

She shook her head, not meeting his eyes.

"What is it?" Something was clearly wrong—why wouldn't she just talk to him?

"I...I don't think I can do this."

He frowned, not understanding. "Do what?"

She gestured at the table, the computer screen, the room in general. "This is just a normal day for you, isn't it?"

Julian tilted his head to the side. "Not exactly normal, but it's not unusual. Why?"

She looked at him then, her eyes brimming with unshed tears. "These are real people." She picked up a piece of paper and waved it. "It was easy for me to look at the names and not go further, but that reporter? He's dead because he tried to do the right thing. Lily's parents are gone. And it looks like the mayor is to blame. If that's true, he's already had people killed. What's to stop him from going after you, too? We recently had a brush with death, but none of it seems to faze you."

Julian's head spun as he tried to decipher what she was really telling him. "If you think I wasn't scared the other night—"

She shook her head, cutting him off. "That's not the issue." She sniffed. "This is just one of your cases.

I know they're not all as dangerous, but I don't know if I can handle you being in harm's way all the time."

"Ruth, it's not like that."

"Oh?" She laughed, but the sound was harsh and cold.

A tingle of dread ran down the valley of his spine. Was she telling him they didn't have a chance? That she didn't want to be with him after all?

"Look, we're both tired," he said. "This has been a rollercoaster of an experience for both of us. Let me get you a hotel room and you can get some rest. Things will be different in the morning." Hopefully a few hours of sleep would help her to see things clearly and she'd realize that things weren't as bad as they currently looked.

"And what will you do?"

"I have a couple more items to check before I meet with the mayor in the morning." He had to make sure his case was strong before he walked into city hall. Ruth had brought up a good point—if they were right, the mayor was a dangerous man. Julian wasn't going to back down, but he also wasn't willing to take unnecessary risks.

Especially not when it might further endanger Ruth.

"I know we need to talk," he continued. "But not right now. Will you give me a little bit of time to settle the case? Then we can figure out where we stand?" Couldn't she just trust him for a little bit longer? Give him a chance to show her his life wasn't always in danger and they could have a future together?

Ruth dropped her gaze, her shoulders slumped. She looked defeated, and Julian's frustration faded as the urge to pull her in for a hug grew stronger.

Finally, she spoke. "All right." She took a deep breath, letting it out in a shuddering sigh. "Don't worry about taking me to a hotel. Just finish your work so you can get some sleep before your meeting tomorrow."

He hated to let her go, but she had a point. Still, there was no way he would leave her unprotected. Not when he was so close to closing this cold case.

"I'll ask someone to drive you," he said. He didn't bother to tell her he'd have a couple of officers stationed in the hotel lobby to intercept anyone who might go looking for her.

Ruth nodded and got to her feet, reaching for her bag. "Will I see you tomorrow?"

Julian nodded. "Count on it."

Julian trotted up the steps of city hall at eight sharp, his sights set on the mayor's office. After Ruth had left last night, he'd spent a few hours digging into the man's publicly available financial ties, and it seemed the mayor had stood to gain quite a lot from the construction of the new convention center. Not only did he have shareholdings with most of the organizations he'd lined up to hold events in the new center, but it looked like he had ties to the construction company, as well. It was all circumstantial evidence at this point, but Julian hoped he could trick the man into revealing something more substantial.

He wished he could have spoken to Ruth this morning. Hopefully she'd gotten some rest and now realized that her fears for him were misplaced. The idea that they might not get to explore this connection between them made his chest ache. He'd love nothing more than to give her his full attention, but he owed it to Lily and her family to focus right now.

Julian walked into the mayor's office and breezed right past his secretary's desk. "Excuse me," the woman said. "You can't go in there."

Julian flashed his badge and a smile. "He's expecting me."

He didn't bother to knock, just opened the door and walked in. "Mr. Mayor," he said. "Good morning."

The man blinked in surprise, but quickly glossed over his reaction with a practiced smile. "Hello, Detective. Nice to see you again."

Julian glanced around, taking in the large office. A wall of windows provided a nice view of Copper Cove, with the Superstition Mountains visible in the far distance. The opposite wall was lined with shelves sporting all manner of memorabilia, from autographed baseballs and framed photographs to a few select books. At the center of it all was the mayor's desk, and the man sitting behind it.

"As I said the other night, I have a few questions about the Gregory and Isabella Pushkin murders." He took a seat without waiting for an invitation.

"Yes. And as I told you, I don't see how I can be helpful."

"With all due respect, I'll be the judge of that," Julian replied.

"Is this going to take long?" the mayor asked. "Because I have a meeting soon, and I'm afraid I must insist—"

"I did some research," Julian said. "And it turns out

you had a lot to gain from the construction of the convention center."

"We all did, Detective," the man replied. "The center has brought many jobs to Copper Cove, and the area around the center is seeing a revitalization."

"I'm sure your bank account is, as well."

"It's not a crime to make money."

Julian shook his head. "Not yet. But I'm curious, because it seems like you also have a connection with the construction company who built the place." He pulled a small notebook from his pocket and pretended to consult it. "It says here a W. Sanderson owns several shares in the company." Julian glanced up. "Mayor Sanderson," he said, using the man's name for the first time. "I know you go by Allen, but isn't your first name William?"

Sanderson narrowed his eyes. "It's a common name."

"If you say so."

"Are we done, Detective?"

Julian tilted his head to the side. "There's just one thing I can't figure out. How do you know Eric Martinez?"

The mayor's face drained of color, confirming Julian's suspicions. "Never mind," Julian said, getting to his feet. "I'll figure it out."

He started for the door, but Sanderson called after him. "You don't know what you're talking about. You have no evidence."

Julian stopped and turned. "Is that what you think?"

"I didn't kill them."

"You may not have pulled the trigger," Julian said, his anger building. "But you're mixed up in this. And it's only a matter of time until I untangle your web."

Sanderson's glare could have stripped paint. "We're done here. Get out."

Julian fired off a mock salute. "See you soon." He turned, then froze as he caught sight of an object on the bookshelves.

A glass sphere, etched with a map of the world.

His mouth went dry as he stared at it, hardly daring to believe his eyes.

"What are you still doing here?" Sanderson snapped.

Julian pointed to the globe. "Where'd you get this?"

"It was a gift," the mayor said, sounding uncertain. "Why?"

"When did you receive it?"

"I don't know." Sanderson shook his head. "It was years ago."

"Six years?" Julian's voice was hoarse, his throat tight.

"Possibly. I don't remember exactly."

He'd heard enough. Julian spun on his heel and reached for the handcuffs fixed to his belt. "Allen Sanderson, you are under arrest for the murders of Gregory and Isabella Pushkin. You have the right to remain silent…"

Chapter Fourteen

Ruth couldn't stop smiling as the officer drove her home. Julian had called her an hour ago and filled her in on his meeting with the mayor and the man's subsequent arrest.

"We did it!" he'd exclaimed. His excitement had been contagious, and despite her lingering worries about their future, a sense of relief had washed over her. "I couldn't have done this without you," he'd said. "I mean it. I owe you everything. Now, go home. I'll have an officer drop you off. You need to rest, and I'm going to be here for the rest of the day."

"It's safe now?" It was what she'd been praying for; had her prayers been answered?

"He's in custody. The news has already spread. Sam messaged me and said the gang is lying low. It's over."

The sense of relief that had washed over Ruth had left her feeling light-headed. After everything that had happened, it was going to be strange to go back to her normal routine. Truth be told, she missed Julian already. But he'd promised to meet her for dinner later. They definitely needed to talk and she was looking forward to figuring out what was going to come next for them.

So she'd climbed into the back of the police car and given the officer directions to her home. What she really wanted was to take a shower and climb directly into bed, but she had a session with Lily this afternoon, and she didn't want to miss this one.

She unlocked the door and stepped inside, glancing around. The air felt stale, a consequence of her having been gone the last few days. The neighbor had kindly taken Morris next door at her request, which meant the house had been empty. At least her plants seemed to have survived her absence.

Ruth hummed as she watered them, her happiness too great to remain contained for long. *Thank You, God.* This nightmare was over, and she and Lily and Julian could go back to their normal lives. Now that they didn't have to worry about looking over their shoulders, she and Julian might be able to move forward with their relationship. It was the best possible outcome, and she was overflowing with gratitude for what the future might hold.

She headed for the bathroom next. The hot water felt good against her still-aching muscles. It turned out being tackled to the ground by a muscular man had its downside. But who was she to complain when they were both still alive?

She dressed quickly, eager to get to her office and see Lily. Ignoring the call of her bed, she headed for the kitchen and the promise of caffeine.

"So you're the therapist."

Ruth spun around so fast she bumped into the lamp

by her sofa and sent it crashing to the floor. Her heart kicked into double time, the blood whooshing loudly in her ears.

A woman stood by her back door, just inside her home. She was well-dressed, her salt-and-pepper hair carefully styled, her makeup flawless.

"Who are you?" Ruth demanded. "This is my house. What do you think you're doing?" She noticed the sparkle of broken glass on the floor by the door. Whoever this was, she must have broken the pane while Ruth was in the shower.

"I'm here to talk to you," the woman replied, stepping forward. "My name is not important." She glanced around, her expression making it clear she didn't think much of Ruth's home. "You know, as a woman living alone you really should invest in better door locks. It didn't take me long to get past that one. Though I can see you don't have much to protect."

"Get out." Ruth moved toward the phone resting on the table. "Now."

The woman made a tsking sound and reached into her bag, pulling out a small gun. "No calls, sweetie. Backup is already on the way."

Panic wrapped around Ruth's throat, making it hard to breathe. "What are you talking about?"

"Don't worry. You'll know soon enough." The woman jerked the gun to the side. "We'll wait in there."

Ruth walked to the kitchen, hyperaware of the gun pointed at her back as she moved.

"Sit."

She did as she was told, and the woman sank onto

a chair on the other side of the table. She was too far away for Ruth to reach, not that she was going to try.

The woman's smile was cold as she regarded Ruth. "You've caused me a lot of trouble. But don't worry. It'll all be over soon."

Something wasn't adding up.

Julian stood in the corner of the interrogation room, listening as Lieutenant Pierce had a turn questioning the mayor.

"Who gave you the globe?"

The mayor's attorney fixed Pierce with a level stare. "As we've already discussed, he doesn't have to answer that."

"I'm just trying to understand," Pierce said. "The globe is being examined in the lab as we speak. It's not the kind of thing that gets cleaned very often, so I'm sure they're going to find Gregory Pushkin's fingerprints on it. We have photos showing that globe on the bookshelf of the Pushkins' home, and we know it was taken the night of the murder. Your client has already admitted to receiving it six years ago. I just want to know who gave it to him."

"And he doesn't have to tell you."

"Who are you protecting?" Julian asked, appealing directly to Sanderson. "As of right now, you're on the hook for these murders. If this really was a gift, that means you didn't kill them. So why not tell us where you got it?"

The mayor met his eyes, but remained silent.

"Your wife," he said, putting it together. "You don't have any children, so she's your only family."

Something flickered in the man's eyes, but he still didn't reply.

"Of course," Julian said to himself. Then fear slammed into him as he realized what that meant.

He pushed out of the interview room, ignoring Pierce's calls. He grabbed his phone and his keys and headed for the parking garage, panic clawing up his throat. "Please, God, keep her safe," he said as he slid behind the wheel of his truck.

He called her number, but she didn't answer. *Please be asleep*, he thought as he sped toward Ruth's place. They were just starting their relationship—he hadn't even had a chance to tell her how he felt yet. Surely God wouldn't take her away from him now?

His tires squealed as he took a hard turn, and someone honked at him. But Julian didn't care. He had to get to her.

Before it was too late.

There was a short knock at her door.

"Come in!" the woman called.

Ruth held her breath as the door opened, already fairly certain as to who was on the other side. Sure enough, two men walked into her home, both sporting yellow-and-black jerseys.

Gang members.

One stepped forward to address the woman, while the other hung back a bit. Ruth caught sight of his face and gasped in surprise.

It was Sam.

He shook his head slightly, warning her not to give him away. She bit her lip and looked away, hoping her reaction hadn't ruined things. Hope flickered to life in her chest, but she dared not nurture it. Sam had stood by while the Pushkins were killed six years ago. She couldn't count on him to help her now.

"She's the one?" the other man said, gesturing to her.

The woman nodded. "You can take care of her first, then go after the girl."

"What were you thinking?"

The woman rolled her eyes. "I don't know. That's your department."

Ruth shrank into her chair as the man looked her over. "What do you think?" he said to Sam. "You up for a breaking and entering gone wrong?"

"It's a classic for a reason," Sam replied.

Her eyes burned with tears as the other man nodded. "Tie her up," he said. "I'll start ransacking the place." He stepped out of the room and seconds later she heard a crash as something broke.

Ruth jerked away as Sam approached. He grabbed her wrists, but his grip wasn't painful. "Let's go," he said, tugging her to her feet. He glanced at the woman, who was still there, watching them.

"You might want to leave for this," he said.

"In a minute," she replied. "I want to watch."

Sam shrugged. "Suit yourself."

He pushed Ruth through the house, back into her bedroom. "Please, don't do this." Her voice broke as he forced her to sit on the bed. "You don't have to hurt me. You can make a different choice."

Julian's face flashed in her mind. Would she ever see him again? She'd let her fear keep her from grabbing a chance at happiness, and now it might be too late to make a different choice. Regret speared through her fear, adding to the chaos of emotion swirling inside her chest.

Sam's expression was apologetic as he slipped a set of zip ties around her wrists. "Trust me," he whispered.

She wanted to, desperately. But her terror was taking over.

The woman stood in the doorway of her room, watching with an air of fascination. "Haven't you seen enough?" Ruth challenged.

"Not yet," she replied. "I'm going to savor this."

Disgust flickered across Sam's face, but since his back was to the woman, she didn't see it. "You should go," he said gruffly. "The longer you're here, the riskier it is for you."

The woman sighed dramatically. "Oh, all right." She sounded disappointed at the prospect of leaving before they killed Ruth. "Just do me a favor. Make it hurt, will you? She deserves it."

Ruth shook her head, her tears falling freely now. Did Sam recall her request, that night he'd broken into her home?

He met her eyes and lifted one eyebrow. "Sure thing, boss."

The faint sounds of destruction carried into her room as the other man continued ransacking her place. The woman turned and left, her footsteps fading down the hall. Sam waited until she was gone before leaning forward.

"I need you to listen to me and do exactly as I say." His voice was low and urgent and Ruth nodded, struggling to focus.

"Good." He opened his mouth to speak again, but the sound of a scream outside cut through the air.

He cursed softly. "What now?"

Footsteps pounded down the hall and the other man burst into her room. "Did you hear that?"

"Yeah," Sam said shortly. He flattened himself against the wall next to her window, peering through the blinds.

"This is the police!" boomed a voice from outside. "Come out with your hands up!"

Ruth choked back a sob as she recognized Julian's voice. He was here! It wasn't too late!

"A cop?" the other man exclaimed. "You've gotta be kidding me."

"It's just one," Sam said. "We've got the advantage."

No! she screamed silently. She could guess what Sam was thinking, and she didn't like it. He might not intend to hurt Julian, but his friend wouldn't hesitate.

"That'll be harder to explain," his partner said. "A dead therapist is one thing. A dead cop is another."

"He's got the boss," Sam said. "What choice do we have?"

"For real?"

Sam nodded, and the other man sighed. "Okay, yeah. We need to move before backup arrives. How do you want to do it?"

"Out the back. Circle the house. We come at him from both sides."

The man glanced at Ruth. "What about her? Should we take care of her first?" Ruth's heart nearly stopped when he reached toward the back waistband of his pants, presumably for his gun.

Sam shook his head. "After. She's not going any-where."

"Make sure you shut her up," the man said. "Can't have her trying to warn him."

Sam glared at him. "Who do you think you're talk-ing to?" He reached over and grabbed a sock off the floor, then stuffed it into her mouth. Ruth tried not to gag. Her panic intensified as breathing got harder, her nose congested from her tears.

"Let's go," Sam said.

"Wait," his partner replied.

"We don't have time," Sam insisted.

"Bring her."

"What?"

He reached out and grabbed Ruth's arm, jerking her off the bed with a painful tug that made her cry out.

"What do you think you're doing?" Sam hissed.

"She's insurance. He won't shoot her. That'll give you time to get the drop on him."

Sam hesitated, then nodded. "Fine. Now let's go."

The man pulled her into the hall. Ruth tried to keep up with them, but her terror made her uncoordinated and she kept stumbling.

They slipped out the back door and into her small yard. She nearly cried out as she watched Sam walk away, but at least she knew he wouldn't hurt Julian. And as for this man? Hopefully he wouldn't hurt her.

"Don't make a sound," he said, his breath hot in her ear. "Cooperate, and I'll make it quick. But if you don't, you'll live just long enough to regret it."

Ruth's blood turned to ice in her veins. *Please, God*, she prayed. *I don't want it to end like this*.

He tugged her again, forcing her to march around the house until they came to the left front corner. The brick was rough against her cheek. She turned her head until she got a bit of the sock stuck on the edge of a brick, then carefully worked it out of her mouth. The man holding her hostage wasn't paying attention to her, so he didn't notice what she'd done.

Ruth took a deep breath for the first time in minutes, grateful for the air. The faint sound of a birdcall floated nearby, and before she knew what was happening, the man pushed her around the corner and forward, keeping one hand on her shoulder and using her for cover as they walked out.

"Hey, is this your girl?" he called loudly.

Julian pivoted to face them, his gun up. Relief flashed across his face when he saw her, but he didn't lower his gun.

"Let her go," he commanded.

"Shoot her!" the woman screamed. Ruth glanced over to find her sitting on the curb, her hands cuffed behind her.

"You hang tight!" the man yelled. "I'll get you in a minute."

Ruth met Julian's eyes. There were so many things she wanted to say to him, but only one mattered right now. *Sam*, she mouthed, trying to tell him about the other man.

Julian frowned, not understanding. She tried again, to no avail.

She spied Sam approaching from behind Julian, creeping closer. It was now or never. "Did you see my cat Sam?" she called loudly.

"What the—" the man behind her exclaimed. He pushed her forward. She tripped over a tree root and fell to the ground, then twisted, looking back at him.

She saw him glance up, notice Sam. Realization dawned on his face. He pointed his gun at her. Ruth tensed, closing her eyes as she braced for the worst.

Gunshots cut through the air with loud booms. He fell on top of her, knocking the breath out of her lungs. She kicked and squirmed, trying to wriggle free.

Then someone grabbed her and pulled her forward, out from under the man's crushing weight. She looked up and caught a glimpse of Julian's face before he drew her to his chest, wrapping his arms around her.

"You're okay," he said, the words coming out in harsh pants of breath.

"So are you." She reached for him, gripping his shirt with her still-bound wrists.

They clung to each other as Sam called for backup and dealt with the woman who'd invaded her home. Ruth wanted to know who she was, but she couldn't bring herself to care at the moment.

"Don't let me go," she whispered to Julian as the sound of sirens drew closer.

"I won't." He pressed a kiss to the top of her head and tightened his embrace. "Not now, not ever."

Epilogue

Six months later

"Come on, Lily!" Ruth yelled from the bleachers. "You can do it!"

Lily turned and searched the crowd. Ruth stood up, waving her arms to draw the girl's attention. Lily saw her and smiled, then turned back to face the pitcher.

The first pitch went wide, but the second was right down the middle. Lily swung, and a crack split the air as her bat made contact with the ball.

Ruth jumped to her feet, screaming with the crowd. She cheered as Lily ran to first base, then on to second. By that time, the outfielder had tossed the ball to third, so she stopped, forced to wait for the next batter's hit before completing her run.

Julian jogged up the bleachers and sat beside her. "What'd I miss?" He leaned over and kissed her cheek, then waved hello to George and Margaret, who were sitting on the other side of Ruth.

"She just made it to second base," Ruth reported. "How'd the meeting go?"

"Good," Julian replied. "Your Dr. Fletcher has some interesting ideas on how the police and counselors can work together to improve the response to mental health calls. I think we're going to form a pilot program and test it out."

She smiled. "I'm glad to hear it."

He stole some of her popcorn. "I suggested you participate."

"You did?" She was flattered by the idea and she felt her cheeks flush.

Julian nodded. "Yeah. I suggested the right kind of music might help defuse a tense situation. Dr. Fletcher thinks it's worth studying, so don't be surprised when he calls you."

"I won't." She was touched to hear Julian had been thinking about the cooperative program, and even more moved to know he'd thought her work worth including.

But his thoughtfulness shouldn't have surprised her. In the six months since arresting the mayor, Julian had proven time and again he was the right man for her. Even though wrapping up the Pushkin murder case had him working long hours, he never missed a chance to have dinner with her, or to spend time with her. He'd even come to church services, and he was now considered a regular by the congregation.

They'd talked a lot about the danger associated with his job. She didn't like the risks, but after everything that had happened, she realized she didn't want to lose any time with him.

Julian had talked about his worries, as well. Ruth

hadn't known it at the time, but when she had decided not to call him after Sam's nocturnal visit, he'd interpreted it as a sign she didn't trust him.

Ruth had met his mother and brother a couple of months ago. Julian had asked her to be there when he told them about his last conversation with his father, and as she'd expected, they hadn't blamed him for his father's death. Ever since that day, Julian had seemed lighter, as though a weight had been removed from his soul.

Watching him work, seeing the tireless way he tied up the loose ends of the case and the way his fellow officers jumped in to assist helped Ruth to let go of the last of her anger toward the police. She was never going to forget the circumstances surrounding her sister's death, but she no longer felt a reflexive sense of distrust when she saw a squad car drive by. No one was perfect, least of all her.

Julian's hand brushed hers as they both reached for popcorn at the same time. A tingle traveled up her arm at the contact. Would there ever come a day when Julian didn't give her butterflies in her stomach? She didn't know, but she was happy to spend the rest of her life trying to find out.

He was the one for her. Ruth felt it in her bones.

He met her gaze and smiled. "Want to grab dinner after this?" he asked. "I know a little Mexican place." There was a twinkle in his eyes that made her laugh.

"I've heard the neighborhood is kind of rough," she teased.

"Don't worry. I'll keep you safe."

Ruth sobered at his words. "I know you will." She

leaned over and kissed him softly on the mouth. "You always do."

He smiled. "So it's a date?"

"I'll go anywhere with you."

His eyes darkened with emotion as he stared down at her. "I don't deserve you."

Ruth laughed. "But you still have me."

"I know. And believe me, I thank God every day."

She smiled up at him. "I love you."

The crowd cheered as the kids on the field made a play. Julian pulled her close and pressed his lips to her ear. "I love you, too. And I'm never letting you go."

Ruth lifted her chin. "Promise?"

He took her hand, and she gasped as something cool and smooth slid down her ring finger. Her eyes filled with tears as she gazed at him, too overwhelmed to speak.

"I do," he said.

* * * * *

Dear Reader,

This is my first book with Love Inspired, and I'm so excited to join this line! I've been thinking about writing this book for a long time, and I'm grateful I got the chance to bring Ruth and Julian's story to life. They've both experienced loss and hardships that have caused their faith to waver, but by working together to help Lily, they renew their faith as they grow to rely on each other. They become true partners, and I enjoyed exploring how their relationship develops over time.

I hope you find their story as compelling as I did!

Happy reading!
Lara

LOVE INSPIRED

Stories to uplift and inspire

Fall in love with Love Inspired—
inspirational and uplifting stories of faith
and hope. Find strength and comfort in
the bonds of friendship and community.
Revel in the warmth of possibility and the
promise of new beginnings.

Sign up for the Love Inspired newsletter
at **LoveInspired.com** to be the first
to find out about upcoming titles,
special promotions and exclusive content.

Get 4 FREE REWARDS!

We'll send you 2 FREE Books plus 2 FREE Mystery Gifts.

FREE
Value Over
$20

Both the **Love Inspired®** and **Love Inspired® Suspense** series feature compelling novels filled with inspirational romance, faith, forgiveness, and hope.

YES! Please send me 2 FREE novels from the Love Inspired or Love Inspired Suspense series and my 2 FREE gifts (gifts are worth about $10 retail). After receiving them, if I don't wish to receive any more books, I can return the shipping statement marked "cancel." If I don't cancel, I will receive 6 brand-new Love Inspired Larger-Print books or Love Inspired Suspense Larger-Print books every month and be billed just $5.99 each in the U.S. or $6.24 each in Canada. That is a savings of at least 17% off the cover price. It's quite a bargain! Shipping and handling is just 50¢ per book in the U.S. and $1.25 per book in Canada.* I understand that accepting the 2 free books and gifts places me under no obligation to buy anything. I can always return a shipment and cancel at any time. The free books and gifts are mine to keep no matter what I decide.

Choose one: ☐ **Love Inspired**
 Larger-Print
 (122/322 IDN GNWC)

☐ **Love Inspired Suspense**
 Larger-Print
 (107/307 IDN GNWN)

Name (please print)

Address   Apt. #

City   State/Province   Zip/Postal Code

Email: Please check this box ☐ if you would like to receive newsletters and promotional emails from Harlequin Enterprises ULC and its affiliates. You can unsubscribe anytime.

> **Mail to the Harlequin Reader Service:**
> **IN U.S.A.:** P.O. Box 1341, Buffalo, NY 14240-8531
> **IN CANADA:** P.O. Box 603, Fort Erie, Ontario L2A 5X3

Want to try 2 free books from another series! Call 1-800-873-8635 or visit www.ReaderService.com.

---

*Terms and prices subject to change without notice. Prices do not include sales taxes, which will be charged (if applicable) based on your state or country of residence. Canadian residents will be charged applicable taxes. Offer not valid in Quebec. This offer is limited to one order per household. Books received may not be as shown. Not valid for current subscribers to the Love Inspired or Love Inspired Suspense series. All orders subject to approval. Credit or debit balances in a customer's account(s) may be offset by any other outstanding balance owed by or to the customer. Please allow 4 to 6 weeks for delivery. Offer available while quantities last.

Your Privacy—Your information is being collected by Harlequin Enterprises ULC, operating as Harlequin Reader Service. For a complete summary of the information we collect, how we use this information and to whom it is disclosed, please visit our privacy notice located at corporate.harlequin.com/privacy-notice. From time to time we may also exchange your personal information with reputable third parties. If you wish to opt out of this sharing of your personal information, please visit readerservice.com/consumerschoice or call 1-800-873-8635. **Notice to California Residents**—Under California law, you have specific rights to control and access your data. For more information on these rights and how to exercise them, visit corporate.harlequin.com/california-privacy.

LIRLIS22

IF YOU ENJOYED THIS BOOK
WE THINK YOU WILL ALSO LOVE

LOVE INSPIRED SUSPENSE
INSPIRATIONAL ROMANCE

Courage. Danger. Faith.

Find strength and determination in stories
of faith and love in the face of danger.

6 NEW BOOKS AVAILABLE EVERY MONTH!

SPECIAL EXCERPT FROM

LOVE INSPIRED SUSPENSE
INSPIRATIONAL ROMANCE

Could a murderer from her past come back to chase her again?

Read on for a sneak preview of
Unsolved Abduction *by Jill Elizabeth Nelson
available April 2022 from Love Inspired Suspense.*

In the darkness of her bedroom, Carina Collins jerked awake, cold sweat coating her body. A scream welled in her throat but remained trapped within her clenched airway. The familiar nightmare always ended in that noiseless scream, just as the memories of her abduction when she was seven years old remained trapped in a deep, dark compartment of her mind. The psychologists said she might never recall what happened. As frustrating as it was to live with a blank spot in her brain, she'd learned to cope.

She lifted her head from her pillow and glanced around the unfamiliar room. Moonbeams stole past the edges of the window blinds and wrapped the space in twilight, barely exposing geometric shapes of unopened boxes squatting against the far wall. Where was she? Oh, right. The move. She and her toddler son, Jace, had relocated from Tulsa to small-town Argyle, Oklahoma, only yesterday.

What had awakened her? Not the dream. A noise. Had Jace cried out?

Carina held her breath and listened. Silence from the direction of Jace's room. No, the sound seemed to float upward from the downstairs floorboards of the small 1950s-era home she'd leased. Surely she was imagining the stealthy tread. But the faint sound was too regular to be the random noises of a house settling. Then that first step at the bottom of the stairs let out its arthritic complaint.

Her pulse stuttered. It hadn't been her nightmare-stirred imagination. Someone was in the house and coming toward her.

Chills cascaded through Carina's body, threatening to paralyze her. She sucked in a breath and shook herself. She was twenty-seven now, not a child, and she had a baby to defend. Carina flung off her covers and sat up. Where was her cell phone? She needed to call for help. Her gut clenched. She'd left the cell downstairs on the charger. Why, oh why, hadn't she brought it up with her when she went to bed? Too late now.

God, please guide me to protect myself and Jace.

Don't miss
Unsolved Abduction *by Jill Elizabeth Nelson*
available wherever Love Inspired Suspense
books and ebooks are sold.

LoveInspired.com

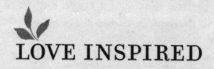